'*Euphoria* is a meticulously researched homage to Mead's restless mind . . . The steam the book emits is as much intellectual as erotic . . . In King's exquisite book, desire – for knowledge, fame, another person – is only fleetingly rewarded'

New York Times

'With *Euphoria*, Lily King gives us a searing and absolutely mesmerizing glimpse into 1930s New Guinea, a world as savage and fascinating as Conrad's *Heart of Darkness*, where obsessions rise to a feverish pitch . . . I loved this book'

Paula McLain, author of *The Paris Wife*

'I have come to expect Lily King's nuanced explorations of the human heart, but in this novel she pulled me in to the exotic world of a woman anthropologist and I was totally captivated'

Karl Marlantes, author of *Matterhorn*

'Persuasive and evocative . . . Finely crafted . . . it shows a talented writer unwilling to settle for what she already does well and eager to give herself new challenges; her ambition is laudable'

Los Angeles Times

'There are some novels that take you by the hand with their lovely prose alone; there are those that pull you in with sensual renderings of time and place and a compelling story; and there are still others that seduce you solely with their subject matter. But it is a rare novel indeed that does all of the above at once and with complete artistic mastery. Yet this is precisely what Lily King has done'

Andre Dubus III, author of *House of Sand and Fog*

'Dazzling . . . an exhilarating novel'   *Boston Globe*

'It's refreshing to see the world's most famous anthropologist brought down to human scale and placed at the centre of this svelte new book'   *Washington Post*

'From Conrad to Kingsolver, the misdeeds of Westerners have inspired their own literary subgenre, and in King's insightful, romantic addition, the work of novelist and anthropologist find resonant parallel: in the beauty and cruelty of others, we discover our own'   *Vogue*

'This impeccably researched story illuminates the state of the world as clearly as the passion of its characters . . . a thrilling read that, at its end, does indeed feel like "the briefest, purest euphoria"'   *Publishers Weekly*

'Masterful . . . A great novelist is like an anthropologist, examining what humans do by habit and custom . . . This is a riveting and provocative novel, absolutely first-rate'
                Seattle Times

'A small gem, disturbing and haunting'   *Kirkus*

EUPHORIA

Also by Lily King

Father of the Rain
The English Teacher
The Pleasing Hour

EUPHORIA

LILY KING

PICADOR

First published 2014 by Atlantic Monthly Press,
an imprint of Grove/Atlantic, Inc., New York

First published in the UK 2014 by Picador
an imprint of Pan Macmillan, a division of Macmillan Publishers Limited
Pan Macmillan, 20 New Wharf Road, London N1 9RR
Basingstoke and Oxford
Associated companies throughout the world
www.panmacmillan.com

ISBN 978-1-4472-8616-5

1 3 5 7 9 8 6 4 2

A CIP catalogue record for this book is available from the British Library.

Printed and bound by CPI Group (UK) Ltd, Croydon, CR0 4YY

For my mother, Wendy,
with all my love

Quarrels over women are the keynote of the New Guinea primitive world.

—Margaret Mead

Experience, contrary to common belief, is mostly imagination.

—Ruth Benedict

1

As they were leaving the Mumbanyo, someone threw something at them. It bobbed a few yards from the stern of the canoe. A pale brown thing.

'Another dead baby,' Fen said.

He had broken her glasses by then, so she didn't know if he was joking.

Ahead lay the bright break in the curve of dark green land where the boat would go. She concentrated on that. She did not turn around again. The few Mumbanyo on the beach were singing and beating the death gong for them, but she did not look at them a last time. Every now and then when the four rowers—all standing, calling back to their people or out to other canoes—pulled at the same time, a small gust of wind struck her damp skin. Her lesions prickled and tightened, as if hurrying to heal in the brief dry air. The wind stopped and started, stopped and started. She could feel the gap between sensation and recognition of it, and knew the fever was coming on again. The rowers ceased rowing to stab a snake-necked turtle and haul it into the boat, still writhing. Behind her, Fen hummed a dirge for the turtle, too low for anyone but her to hear.

A motorboat was waiting for them where the Yuat met the Sepik. There were two white couples on board with the driver, a man named Minton whom Fen knew from Cairns.

The women wore stiff dresses and silk stockings, the men dinner jackets. They did not complain about the heat, which meant they lived here, the men overseeing either plantations or mines, or enforcing the laws that protected them. At least they weren't missionaries. She couldn't have tolerated a missionary today. One woman had bright gold hair, the other eyelashes like black ferns. Both carried beaded purses. The smooth white of their arms looked fake. She wanted to touch the one closer to her, push up her sleeve and see how far up the white went, the way all her tribes wherever she went needed to touch her when she first arrived. She saw pity in the women's gazes as she and Fen boarded with their dirty duffels and their malarial eyes.

The engine when it started up was so loud, so startling, that her hands rose to her ears like a child's. She saw Fen flinch to do the same and she smiled reflexively, but he did not like that she'd noticed and moved away from her to talk to Minton. She took a seat on the bench at the stern with the women.

'What's the occasion?' she asked Tillie, the gold-haired one. If she'd had that hair, the natives would never have stopped touching. You couldn't go into the field with hair like that.

They both managed to hear her over the engine and laughed.

'It's Christmas Eve, silly.'

They had been drinking already, though it couldn't have been much past noon, and it would have been easier to be called silly if she hadn't been wearing a filthy cotton shift over Fen's pajamas. She had the lesions, a fresh gash on her hand

2

from a sago palm thorn, a weakness in her right ankle, the old Solomon neuritis in her arms, and an itchy sting between her toes that she hoped wasn't another batch of ringworm. She could normally keep the discomfort at bay while she was working but it kicked in hard watching these women in their silks and pearls.

'Do you think Lieutenant Boswell will be there?' Tillie asked the other woman.

'She thinks he's divine.' This one, Eva, was taller, stately, bare-fingered.

'I do not. And so do you,' Tillie said.

'But *you* are a married woman, my dear.'

'You can't expect someone to stop noticing people the minute the ring goes on,' Tillie said.

'I don't. But your husband certainly does.'

In her mind Nell was writing:

—ornamentation of neck, wrists, fingers
—paint on face only
—emphasis on lips (dark red) and eyes (black)
—hips emphasized by cinching of waist
—conversation competitive
—the valued thing is the man, not having one, neces-
    sarily, but having the ability to attract one

She couldn't stop herself.

'Have you been studying the natives?' Tillie asked her.

'No, she's come from the Twilight Ball at the Floating Palais.' Eva had the heavier Australian accent, the most like Fen's.

3

'I have,' she said. 'Since July. I mean, the July before this last one.'

'A *year and a half* up that little tributary somewhere?' Tillie said.

'Good God,' Eva said.

'A year first in the mountains north of here with the Anapa,' Nell said. 'And then another five and a half months with the Mumbanyo up the Yuat. We left early. I didn't like them.'

'*Like* them?' Eva said. 'I would think keeping your head attached to your neck might be a more reasonable goal.'

'Were they cannibals?'

It was not safe to give them an honest answer. She did not know who their men were. 'No. They fully understand and abide by the new laws.'

'They're not *new*,' Eva said. 'They were issued four years ago.'

'I think to an ancient tribe it all feels new. But they obey.' And blame all their bad luck on the lack of homicide.

'Do they talk about it?' Tillie said.

She wondered why every white asked about cannibalism. She thought of Fen when he returned from the ten-day hunt, his sad attempt to keep it from her. I tasted it, he finally blurted out. And they're right, it does taste like old pig. It was a joke the Mumbanyo had, that the missionaries had tasted like old pig.

'They speak of it with great longing.'

The two women, even long brazen Eva, shrank a bit.

And then Tillie asked, 'Did you read the book about the Solomon Islands?'

4

'Where all the children were fornicating in the bushes?'

'Eva!'

'I did.' And then, Nell couldn't help herself, 'Did you like it?'

'Oh I don't know,' Tillie said. 'I don't understand what all the fuss is about.'

'Is there fuss?' Nell said. She'd heard nothing about its reception in Australia.

'I'll say.'

She wanted to ask by whom and about what, but one of the men was coming around with an enormous bottle of gin, refilling glasses.

'Your husband said you wouldn't want any,' he said to her apologetically, for he did not have a glass for her.

Fen had his back to her but she could see the expression on his face just from the way he was standing with his back arched and his heels slightly lifted. He would be compensating for his wrinkled clothing and his odd profession with a hard masculine glare. He would allow himself a small smile only if he himself had made the joke.

Fortified by several sips, Tillie continued her inquiry. 'And what will you write about these tribes?'

'It's all a jumble in my head still. I never know anything until I get back to my desk in New York.' She was aware of her own impulse to compete, to establish dominance over these clean, pretty women by conjuring up a desk in New York.

'Is that where you're headed now, back to your desk?'

Her desk. Her office. The diagonal window that looked out onto Amsterdam and 118th. Distance could feel like a terrible claustrophobia at times. 'No, we're going to Victoria next, to study the Aborigines.'

Tillie pulled a pout. 'You poor thing. You look beat up enough as it is.'

'We can tell you right here all you need to know about the Abos,' Eva said.

'It was just this last five months, this last tribe.' She could not think how to describe them. She and Fen had not agreed on one thing about the Mumbanyo. He had stripped her of her opinions. She marveled now at the blankness. Tillie was looking at her with a drunk's depthless concern. 'Sometimes you just find a culture that breaks your heart,' she said finally.

'Nellie,' Fen called at her. 'Minton says Bankson is still here.' He waved his hand upriver.

Of course he is, she thought, but said, 'The one who stole your butterfly net?' She was trying to be playful.

'He didn't steal anything.'

What had he said exactly? It had been on the ship coming home from the Solomons, in one of their first conversations. They'd been gossiping about their old professors. Haddon liked me, Fen had said, but he gave Bankson his butterfly net.

Bankson had ruined their plans. They'd come in '31 to study two New Guinea tribes. But because Bankson was on the Sepik River, they'd gone north, up the mountains to the Anapa, with the hope that when they came back down in a year he'd be gone and they'd have their pick of the river tribes, whose less isolated cultures were rich with artistic, economic, and spiritual traditions. But he was still there, so they'd gone in the opposite direction from him and the Kiona he studied, south down a tributary of the Sepik called the Yuat, where they'd found the Mumbanyo. She had known that tribe was a mistake after the first week, but it took her five months to convince Fen to leave.

Fen stood beside her. 'We should go and see him.'

'Really?' He'd never suggested this before. Why now, when they'd already made arrangements for Australia? He had been with Haddon, Bankson, and the butterfly net in Sydney four years ago, and she didn't think they had liked each other much.

Bankson's Kiona were warriors, the rulers of the Sepik before the Australian government had cracked down, separating villages, allotting them parcels of land they did not want, throwing resisters in jail. The Mumbanyo, fierce warriors themselves, told tales of the Kiona's prowess. This was why he wanted to visit Bankson. The tribe is always greener on the other side of the river, she often tried to tell him. But it was impossible not to be envious of other people's people. Until you laid it all out neatly on the page, your own tribe looked a mess.

'Do you think we'll see him in Angoram?' she asked. They could not go traipsing after Bankson. They'd made the decision to go to Australia. Their money wouldn't last much more than half a year, and it would take several weeks to get settled among the Aborigines.

'Doubt it. I'm sure he steers clear of the government station.'

The speed of the boat was disorienting. 'We need to get that pinnace to Port Moresby tomorrow, Fen. The Gunai are a good choice for us.'

'You thought the Mumbanyo were a good choice for us, too, when we headed there.' He rattled the ice of his empty glass. He looked like he had more to say, but he walked back to Minton and the other men.

'Been married long?" asked Tillie.

'Two years in May,' Nell said. 'We had the ceremony the day before we came out here.'

'Swish honeymoon.'

They laughed. The bottle of gin came round again.

For the next four and a half hours Nell watched the dressed-up couples drink, tease, flirt, wound, laugh, apologize, separate, reintegrate. She watched their young uneasy faces, saw how thin the layer of self-confidence was, how easily it slipped off when they thought no one was looking. Occasionally Tillie's husband would raise his arm to point out something on land: two boys with a net, a quoll hanging like a melting sack from a tree, an osprey coasting to its nest, a red parrot mocking their engine. She tried not to think about the villages they were passing, the raised houses and the fire pits and the children hunting for snakes in the thatch with spears. All the people she was missing, the tribes she would never know and words she would never hear, the worry that they might right now be passing the one people she was meant to study, a people whose genius she would unlock, and who would unlock hers, a people who had a way of life that made sense to her. Instead she watched these Westerners and she watched Fen, speaking his hard talk to the men, aggressively pressing them about their work, defensively responding when they asked about his, coming to seek her out then punishing her with a few cutting words and an abrupt retreat. He did this four or five times, dumping his frustration on her, unaware of his own pattern. He was not through punishing her for wanting to leave the Mumbanyo.

'He's handsome, isn't he, your husband,' Eva said, when no one else could hear. 'I bet he cleans up well.'

The boat slowed, the water glowed salmon pink in the sunset, and they were there. Three dock boys, dressed in white pants, blue shirts, and red caps came running out from the Angoram Club to tie up the boat.

'Lukaut long,' Minton barked at them in pidgin. 'Isi isi.'

To each other they spoke in their tribal language, Taway most likely. To the disembarking passengers they said, 'Good evening,' in a crisp British accent. She wondered how far their knowledge of English extended.

'How are you this evening?' she asked the biggest boy.

'Fine, thank you, Madame.' He reminded her of their Anapa shoot boy, with his easy confidence and willingness to smile.

'It's Christmas Eve, I hear.'

'Yes, Madame.'

'Do you celebrate it?'

'Oh yes, Ma'am.'

The missionaries had gotten to them.

'And what are you hoping for?' she asked the second biggest.

'A fishing net, Ma'am.' He tried to keep the sentence brief and dispassionate like the other boy's, but he burst out, 'Like the one my brother has got last year.'

'And the first thing he catched were me!' the littlest cried out.

All three boys laughed, their teeth bright white. At their age most Mumbanyo boys no longer had many teeth, having lost them to rot or fights, and the ones that remained were stained scarlet by the betel nut they chewed.

Just as the big boy began to explain, Fen called to her from the ramp. The white couples, already up on the land, seemed to be laughing at them, at the woman in the filthy men's pajamas, trying to talk to the natives, at the gaunt bearded Aussie, who may or may not clean up well, teetering with their bags, calling for his wife.

She told the boys to have a merry Christmas, which they thought was funny, and they wished her the same. She would have liked to squat on that dock with those boys all night.

Fen, she saw, was not mad. He shifted both bags onto his left shoulder and offered her his right arm as if she too were wearing an evening dress. She slipped her left arm through and he clamped down. The lesion she had there stung from the pressure.

'It's Christmas Eve for Christ's sake. Must you always be working?' But his voice was teasing now, almost apologetic. We are here, his arm tight around hers said. It is over with the Mumbanyo. He kissed her and this too made the pain flare but she didn't complain. He didn't like her strong, nor did he like her weak. Many months ago he'd grown tired of sickness and sores. When his fever rose, he took forty-mile hikes. When he had a thick white worm growing beneath the skin of his leg, he cut it out himself with a penknife.

They were given a room on the second story. Music from the club's dining room below vibrated in the floorboards.

She touched one of the twin beds. It was made up with stiff white sheets and a fat pillow. She pulled the top sheet from its tight bind and got in. It was just an old narrow army cot but it felt like a cloud, a clean smooth starched cloud. She felt sleep, the old heavy kind, the kind of her childhood, come for her.

'Good idea,' Fen said, taking off his shoes. There was a whole bed for him, too, but he pushed his way in beside her and she had to turn toward him on her side so as not to fall off. 'Time to procreate,' he said in a singsong.

His hands slid down the back of her cotton pants, grabbed the flesh of her bottom, and pressed her groin to his. It reminded her of how she used to smack her paper dolls together after she had outgrown them but had not yet put them away. But it didn't work, so he took her hand and brought it down and once she had gripped him fully, he covered her hand with his own and brought it up and down in a rhythm she knew well but he would never let her try on her own. His breathing quickly became fast and labored, but it took a long time for the penis to show even the slightest sign of stiffness. It flopped beneath their two hands like a jellyfish. It wasn't the right time, anyway. She was about to get her period.

'Shit,' Fen muttered. 'Bloody hell.'

The anger seemed to send a surge of something down there, and suddenly it shot out of their hands, huge, hard, and flushed purple.

'Stick it in,' Fen said. 'Stick it in right now.'

There was no reasoning with him, no speaking of dryness or timing or oncoming fevers or lesions that would open when rubbed against the linen sheets. They would leave bloody stains and the Taway maids would think it was menstrual blood and have to burn them for superstitious reason, these beautiful fresh clean sheets.

She stuck it in. The small sections of her flesh that did not hurt were numb if not dead. Fen pumped against her.

When it was over, he said, 'There's your baby.'

'At least a leg or two,' she said, as soon as she could trust her voice.

He laughed. The Mumbanyo believed it took many times to make a whole baby. 'We'll get to the arms later tonight.' He swiveled his face to hers and kissed her. 'Now let's get ready for that party.'

There was an enormous Christmas tree in the far corner. It looked real, as if they'd shipped it from New Hampshire. The room was crowded with men mostly, owners and overseers, river drivers and government kiaps, crocodile hunters with their smelly taxidermists, traders, smugglers, and a few hard-drinking ministers. The pretty women from the boat seemed to glow, each at the center of her own ring of men. Taway servants wore white aprons and carried trays of champagne. They had long limbs and long, narrow noses, unmarked by piercings or scarring. They were, she guessed, a nonwarring people like the Anapa. What would happen if they ever put a governor's station down the Yuat River? You couldn't tie a white apron on a Mumbanyo. You'd get your neck slit if you tried.

She took a glass from a tray held out to her. On the other side of the room, beyond the tray and the arm of the

Taway man who held it, she saw a man beside the tree, a man quite possibly taller than the tree, touching a branch with his fingers.

Without her glasses, my face would have been little more than a pinkish smudge among many, but she seemed to know it was me as soon as I lifted my head.

2

Three days earlier, I'd gone to the river to drown myself.

Are you serious, Andy? The question beat through my body at regular intervals, sometimes in my own voice, sometimes in one of my brothers': Martin's full of the irony of the situation, John's more concerned but still with a bit of an eyebrow raised. There was a thinness to the air as I moved through the bush beyond my village, northwest, toward an empty spot on the water. A few steps closer to London, just a few. Hello, Mum; goodbye, Mum. I loved you, I did, before you drove me out of the bleeding hemisphere. I wasn't sure I was taking in oxygen. I couldn't feel my tongue. *He cain't feel his tongue, wha?* I could hear Martin call to John in the voice of our old cook Mary. John was laughing too much to answer. The stones were ridiculous, and clacked loudly against my thighs. Now my brothers were laughing at the linen jacket, our father's, the one that had the egg stain Martin would be remembering. *He had a proper fit, didn't he, Andy, when I kindly brought the splodge to his attention.* I swatted through the thick growth, my brothers miming me, exaggerating me behind my back, John telling Martin to stop making him laugh or he'd piss. I came to the place where Teket's boy had been bitten by a death adder. He died quickly—the respiratory system shuts down entirely. Some chaps have all the luck, eh? Martin said. Funny how when you have a purpose the misery goes and hides. The feeling that had clung to me like wax for so long was gone, and I felt strangely buoyant, my humor returned to me, my brothers closer than they had felt in years. Almost as if they were about to truly speak again. Perhaps all suicides are happy in the end. Perhaps it is at that moment that one feels the real point of it all, which, after you get yourself born, is to die. It is the one thing each and every one of us is programmed for, directed to, and cannot swerve away from indefinitely. Even my father, also dead, would have to agree with that. Was this how Martin felt marching toward Piccadilly? That's how I'd always imagined it, not walking or running but marching, marching like John marching to the war that ate him. And then the gun, from his pocket to his ear. Not his temple, but his ear. They had made that clear, for some reason. As if he had just meant to stop hearing, not stop living. Had the metal touched skin? Had he paused to feel the cold of it or was it all done in one moment, one smooth gesture? Had he laughed? I could only see Martin laughing at that moment. Nothing had ever been particularly serious to Martin. Certainly not a young man in Piccadilly with a gun to his ear. That's what bothered me so much when I heard, when the headmaster came and fetched me from French class. Why had Martin been so serious about that one thing? Couldn't he have been serious about something else? I felt the slough coming back now, a sort of mental suffocation. Old Prall in my office would get the news and he would feel as I had done that day in the headmaster's room, staring at a fern on the windowsill and doubting that Martin had been serious. Prall would hardly know whether to laugh or cry. Bloody Bankson's gone and drowned himself in that river, he'd sputter to Maxley or Henin down the hall. And then someone would laugh. How could they not? But I could not go back and sit in that mosquito room alone again. If I did not turn toward the river (it was glinting now through the waxy green platter-sized leaves) I'd just have to keep walking. Eventually I'd reach the Pabei. I'd never met one. Half of them had been calaboosed because they wouldn't abide by the new laws.

I headed toward the water. I bit hard on the muscle of my tongue. Harder. I could not feel it, though the blood came, metal, inhuman. I walked straight into the river. Yes, it had probably been all one gesture, out of the pocket and to the ear and bang. The water was warm and the linen jacket did not float up. It hung heavy and tight against me. I heard movement behind me. A crocodile perhaps. For the first time I felt no fear of them. Eaten by a croc. Tops blowing your head off in Piccadilly Circus. Crocodiles were sacred to the Kiona. Perhaps I would become part of their mythology, the unhappy white man who became a crocodile. I went under. My mind was not still but I was not unhappy. Unfortunately I'd always been able to hold my breath. We used to compete, Martin, John, and I. They thought it was funny that the youngest had the biggest lungs, that I passed out before giving up. You're part fainting goat, Andy, my father often said.

They grabbed me so hard and fast I took in water and, though I was in the air again, I couldn't breathe. Each man had hooked an arm around my shoulder. They dragged me to shore, flipped me over, pounded me like a sago pancake, and pulled me back up to standing, all the while lecturing me in their language. They found the stones in my pocket. They grabbed them, the two men, their bodies nearly dry already for they wore nothing but rope around their waists while I sagged with the weight of all my clothes. They made a pile of the stones from my pockets on the beach and shifted language to a Kiona worse than mine, explaining that they knew I was Teket's man from Nengai. The stones are beautiful, they said, but dangerous. You can collect them, but leave them on land before you swim. And do not swim in clothes. This is also dangerous. And do not swim alone. Being alone you will only come to harm. They asked me if I knew the way back. They were stern and curt. Grown-ups who didn't have patience for an oversized child.

'Yes,' I told them, 'I am fine.'

'We cannot go further.'

'That is fine.'

I began walking back. I heard them behind me, return-ing upriver. They were speaking quickly, loudly, in Pabei. I heard a word I knew, taiku, the Kiona word for stones. One said it then the other said it, louder. Then loud belly-shaking guffaws of laughter. They laughed like people in England used to laugh before the war, when I was a boy.

I was going to be alive for Christmas after all, so I packed a bag and went to spend it with the drunks at the Government Station in Angoram.

3

'Bankson. Christ. Good to lay eyes on you, man.'

I remembered Schuyler Fenwick as a chippy, tightly wound suck-arse who didn't like me much. But when I put out my hand he pushed it aside and wrapped his arms around me. I hugged him in return and this display got a good laugh from the sloshed kiaps nearby. My throat burned with the unexpected emotion of it, and I didn't have time to recover before he introduced me to his wife.

'It's Bankson,' he said, as if I were all they talked of, night and day.

'Nell Stone,' she said.

Nell Stone? Fen had married Nell Stone? He was one for tricks, but this seemed to be in earnest.

No one had ever mentioned, in all the talk of Nell Stone, that she was so slight, or sickly. She offered me a hand with a thinly healed gash across the palm. To take it would mean causing her discomfort. Her smile bloomed naturally but the rest of her face was sallow and her eyes seemed coated over by pain. She had a small face and large smoke-colored eyes like a cuscus, the small marsupial Kiona children kept as pets.

'You're hurt.' I nearly said *ill*. I touched her hand loosely, briefly.

'Wounded but not slain.' She managed something close to a laugh. Lovely lips in a devastatingly tired face.

I will lay me down for to bleed awhile, the ballad went on in my head. *Then I'll rise and fight with you again.*

'How fantastic that you're still here,' Fen said. 'We thought you might have left by now.'

'I should have done. I think my Kiona would celebrate for a week straight if I pissed off. But there's always that one last piece to shove in place, even if it's the wrong shape entirely.'

They laughed heavily, a sort of deeply sympathetic agreement that was like a salve on my shredded nerves.

'It always feels like that in the field, doesn't it?' Nell said. 'Then you get back and it all fits.'

'Does it?' I said.

'If you've done the work it will.'

'Will it?' I needed to get the barmy edge out of my voice. 'Let's get more drinks. And food. Do you want food? Of course you must. Shall we sit?' My heart whapped in my throat and all I could think was how to keep them, how to keep them. I felt my loneliness bulge out of me like a goiter, and I wasn't sure how to hide it from them.

There were a few empty tables at the back of the room. We headed for the one in the corner through a cloud of tobacco smoke, squeezed between a group of white patrol officers and gold prospectors drinking fast and shouting at each other. The band started up with "Lady of Spain" but no one danced. I stopped a waiter, pointed to the table, and asked him to bring us dinner. They walked ahead of me, Fen first, far in front, for Nell was slowed by a limp in her left ankle. I walked close behind her. The back of her blue cotton dress was bent with wrinkles.

Nell Stone, to my mind, was older, matronly. I hadn't read the book that had recently made her famous, the book that made the mention of her name conjure up visions of salacious behavior on tropical beaches, but I'd pictured an American hausfrau amid the sexual escapades of the Solomons. This Nell Stone, however, was nearly a girl, with thin arms and a thick plait down her back.

We settled in at the little table. A sorry portrait of the King loomed above us.

'Where have you come from?' I said.

'We started in the mountains,' Nell said.

'The highlands?'

'No, the Torricelli.'

'A year with a tribe that had no name for themselves.'

'We named them after their little mountain,' Nell said. 'Anapa.'

'If they had been *dead* they would have been less boring,' Fen said.

'They were very sweet and gentle, but malnourished and weak.'

'Asphyxiatingly dull, you mean,' Fen said.

'Fen was basically out on hunts for a year.'

'It was the only way to stay awake.'

'I spent my days with the women and children in the gardens, growing just barely enough for the village.'

'And you've just come from there?' I was trying to piece together where and how she'd got in such rough shape.

'No, no. We left them in—?' Fen turned to her.

'July.'

'Came down and crept a little closer to you. Found a tribe down the Yuat.'

'Which?'

'The Mumbanyo.'

I hadn't heard of them.

'Fearsome warriors,' Fen said. 'Give your Kiona a run for it, I'd bet. Terrorized every other tribe up and down the Yuat. And each other.'

'And us,' Nell said.

'Just you, Nellie.' Fen said.

The waiter brought our food: beef, mash, and thick yellow English wax beans— the type I'd hoped never in my life to see again. We gorged on the meat and conversation all at once, not bothering to cover our mouths or wait our turn. We interrupted and interjected. We pummeled each other, though perhaps they, being two, did more of the pummeling. From the nature of their questions—Fen's about religion and religious totems, ceremonies, warfare, and genealogy; Nell's about economics, food, government, social structure, and child-rearing—I could tell they'd divided their areas neatly, and I felt a stab of envy. In every letter I'd written to my department at Cambridge, I'd asked for a partner, some young fellow just starting out in need of a little guidance. But everyone wanted to stake out his own territory. Or perhaps, though I took great pains to conceal it, they'd sensed in my letters the mire of my thoughts, the stagnation of my work, and stayed away.

'What have you done to your foot?' I asked her.

'I sprained it going up the Anapa.'

'What, seventeen months ago?'

'They had to carry her up on a pole,' Fen said, amused by the memory.

'They wrapped me in banana leaves so I looked like a trussed-up pig they were planning to have for dinner.' She

21

and Fen laughed, sudden and hard, as if they'd never laughed about it before.

'A good part of the time I was upside down,' she said. 'Fen went on ahead and got there a day earlier and never sent so much as a note back to me. It took them over two hundred porters to get all our equipment up there.'

'I was the only one with a gun,' Fen said. 'They warned us that ambushes were not uncommon. Those tribes are starving up there, and we were carrying all our food.'

'It must be broken,' I said.

'What?'

'Your ankle.'

'Yes'—she looked at Fen, cautiously I thought—'I suppose so.'

I saw then she hadn't eaten as he and I had done. The food had just been pushed around her plate.

A chair fell over behind me. Two kiaps gripped each other by their government uniforms, red-faced and staggering like drunken dance partners, until one of them pulled his arm out and swung back a fist fast and hard against the other man's mouth. By the time they were pulled apart their faces looked as if they'd been dug up with a garden claw and their hands were covered with each other's blood. Voices swelled, and the leader of the band encouraged everyone to dance, striking up a quick loud tune. But no one paid any attention. Another fight broke out on the other side of the room.

'Let's go,' I said.

'Go? Where to?' Fen said.

'I'll take you upriver. Plenty of room at my place.'

'We have a room upstairs,' Nell said.

'You won't sleep. And if they burn the place down, you won't have a bed. This lot have been drinking steadily for five days now.' I pointed to her hand and the lesions I'd just noticed on her left arm. 'And I have medicine for those cuts. They don't look like they've been treated at all.'

I was standing now, hovering, waiting for them to agree. Whap whap. I need you. I need you. I changed tacks, said to Fen, 'You said you'd like to see the Kiona.'

'I would, very much. But we're leaving for Melbourne in the morning.'

'How's that?' There had been no mention of leaving New Guinea in the several hours we'd been together.

'We're going to try and steal a tribe from Elkin.'

'No.' I didn't mean to say it, not in such a petulant tone. 'Why?' The Aborigines? They couldn't go to the Aborigines. 'What about the Mumbanyo? You've only been there five months.'

Fen looked at Nell to explain.

'We couldn't stay any longer,' she said. '*I* couldn't at any rate. And we had the idea that maybe in Australia we could find a region that has not been claimed.'

The word *claimed* helped me to understand. I suspect she knew it would. 'Do not under any circumstances leave the Sepik because of me. I do not own it, nor do I want to. There are eighty anthropologists for every bloody Navajo, yet they give me a seven-hundred-mile river. No one dares come near. They think it's "mine." I don't want it!' I was aware of the whinge in my voice. I didn't care. I'd get on my knees if I had to. 'Please stay. I will find you a tribe tomorrow—there are hundreds of them—far far away from me if you like.'

They agreed so quickly, and without even glancing at each other, that I wondered afterward if they'd been playing me rather handily all along. It didn't matter. They might have needed me. But I needed them far more.

As I waited for them to collect their things from their upstairs room, I tried to recall every tribe I'd heard of up and down the river. The first that came to mind was the Tam. My informant, Teket, had a cousin who'd married a Tam and he always used the word peaceful when he described his time there. I'd seen a few Tam women trading their fish at market and I'd noted their laconic business savvy, the way they held their ground against the hard-bargaining Kiona where other tribes capitulated. But Lake Tam was too far. I needed to think of a people much closer.

They came down with their bags.

'That can't be all you've got.'

Fen grinned. 'No, not quite.'

'We sent the rest on to Port Moresby,' Nell said. She had changed into a man's white shirt and tan trousers, as if she expected to be back at work by morning.

'I can send word to have it brought back up. That is, if you stay.' I picked up two of their duffels and headed out before they could change their mind.

My ears rung in the sudden quiet. With the electric light pouring out of the government house and the music tapering to a thin strain and the shorn grass underfoot, we could have been walking out of a dance at Cambridge on a warm night. I turned back and Fen had taken her hand.

I led them across the road, past the docks, through the break in a thicket, and onto the small beach where I'd stashed my canoe. Even in the dark I could see their faces droop. I think they'd imagined a proper boat, with seats and cushions.

'I won this. It's a war canoe. I got it for shooting a boar.' I made up for their disappointment with great energy, tossing their bags in then running back up the beach for the engine, which I had hid behind a fat fig tree.

They brightened up considerably when they saw it. They'd thought I was going to paddle them to my village, which would have taken all night and most of the next morning.

'Now this is something I haven't seen,' Fen said as I bolted the motor into place.

I rearranged the duffels at the front, making a bed of sorts so Nell could sleep. I directed her toward it, put Fen in the middle, and pushed us out a few yards. After I hopped in I pulled the cord and hit the throttle hard. If they had any last doubts I didn't hear them over the wail of the engine, which slid us quickly across the dark crimped water toward Nengai.

4

I was raised on Science as other people are raised on God, or gods, or the crocodile.

If you took aim at New Guinea and shot an arrow up through the globe, it might come out the other side at the village of Grantchester, on the outskirts of Cambridge, England. The house I grew up in there, Hemsley House, had been in the possession of Bankson scientists for three generations, its every desktop, drawer, and wardrobe stuffed with science's remnants: spyglasses, test tubes, finger scales, pocket magnifiers, loupes, compasses, and a brass telescope; boxes of glass slides and ento pins, geodes, fossils, bones, teeth, petrified wood, framed beetles and butterflies, and thousands of loose insect carcasses that turned to powder upon contact.

My father read zoology in St. John's College at Cambridge and became a fellow and steward there as was expected. He and my mother met in 1897, married that June, and had three boys three years apart: John then Martin then me.

My father had a big moustache, which often hid a small smile. I didn't understand his humor until I was grown and he had lost it, and took him very much at his word, which amused him, too. He was interested, for my entire childhood, in eggs. He incubated them first in Nanny's room then, when she complained, out in a shed. When they were ready he'd pick up each egg, write down the number of the pen, hen, and date of laying, then pick off the shell and study every detail of the embryo. He bred mice, pigeons, guinea pigs, goats, and rabbits; he grew and studied snapdragons and peas. He never lost his passion for Mendel. He believed there was a missing piece to Darwin's theories, as did Darwin himself, for there had to be an explanation of how phenotypes were transferred from one generation to the next. His concept of genetics began with an image of a wave or a vibration. His career—piebald as it was, sometimes pariah, sometimes hero—was the result of his curiosity, his interrogative nature. He was an apostle of science, of the pursuit of questions and answers, and he expected his sons to be apostles, too.

By the time I reached New Guinea in 1931, when I was twenty-seven, my mother and I were the only remaining members of our family, and she had become a great psychological burden to me, both needy and despotic, a tyrant who seemed not to know what she wanted for or from her last remaining subject. But she had not always been so. In my youth I remember her as soft and sweet and, though I was the last of the lot, young. I remember her deferring to my father in all instances, waiting for his word on one matter or the other, unable to give us boys answers to the most benign of questions: Could we bring the spiders in the house if they were in jars? Could we spread jam on the rock to watch the slave-maker ants try and transport it? We had a special bond because she did not want me to grow up and I did not want to grow up either. My brothers didn't make it look easy. John agreed to everything my father said, and Martin next to nothing. Neither

27

road looked all that sunny to me, so I was happy to sprawl in my mother's lap for a good long time.

Our visit to my father's sister, Aunt Dottie, in the summer of 1910 is the first sustained memory I have. She was one of our many maiden aunts, and the most interesting to me. She had an exquisite beetle collection, all pinned and framed and labeled in her copperplate, squares and squares of them, laid out on velvet. Other women had jewelry; Aunt Dottie had beetles in every color and shape, all found in the New Forest, which was ten miles from her house. It was to the New Forest we would go every day with her in our gumboots and our buckets knocking together. There was a pond she liked, a good hour's walk in, and she'd be the first to march straight in it, the mud sometimes deeper than her wellies, and more than once we had to pull her out, all three of us in a line—me at the end on dry ground—and laughing too hard to be of any use, but Aunt Dottie would play it up, pretending to be stuck and sinking and then allowing us to slowly bring her up and out of the water. She always had the most stunning creatures in her net—a natterjack toad, a great-crested newt, a swallowtail butterfly—and could only be rivaled occasionally by John, who had more patience than Martin or me with our scoopfuls of tadpoles. That is where my mind goes when I think of John, twelve years old, wading into a steaming, buzzing pond in the New Forest on a hot July day, bucket in one hand, net in the other, his eyes scouring the filmy surface. We got a letter after he died from a fellow officer who said John treated the war like a good long field excursion. 'I do not mean to imply that he was not focused when he needed to be; he was, as I'm sure you have learnt from his commanding officers, an exceptionally courageous and thoughtful soldier. But while his comrades were inclined to complain about living in a ten-foot ditch, John would let out a jubilant yelp, having found the fossil of a Pliocene mollusk or spied a rare species of falcon flying overhead. He had a great passion for this earth, and while he left it and us far too soon, I am certain he is home.' My mother did not like this letter or its suggestion that John was 'home' when his body was blown to bits over a Belgian farm, but I took comfort in it. There was little comfort after John's death, and I chose to take it where I could find it.

John had the most potential to fulfill my father's wishes for us. He was a passionate naturalist. His identification of an extremely rare caterpillar when he was fifteen made it into *The Entomologist's Record*. He took the prize in biology in his final year at Charterhouse School. If the war had not inter-rupted his trajectory, he would have most likely gone on to become the fourth Bankson to be a Cambridge don. At least this is what we all tell ourselves. John would have placated Father, and Martin would have been at liberty to follow his fancies. But John did not want to kill the things he studied. Nor was he interested in eggs or peas or cells or what they were calling germ plasma. He was interested in the triple-jointed legs of beetles and the eclipse feathers of mallards. He wanted to be outside mucking about in a field. But there's no need to quibble over John. He is gone, as is all his potential and his happy little yelp in the trenches of Rosières as he dug a fossil out of the hard dirt wall.

Martin tried to appease my father and my father's ter-rible grief after John died by studying biology, zoology, and organic chemistry. Only on the side, on the sly, would he write a poem or a play. But his grades were poor and he was miserable and finally he had to tell my father the truth. He was more interested in creating literature. My father was a great reader and a lover of the arts; he took us to the British Museum and the Tate and he read Blake and Tennyson to us in the evenings when we were children. But he did not believe ordinary citizens created art. True art was anomalous; it was a rare mutation. It didn't happen simply because one willed it so. He thought it an utter and exasperating waste of an ordinary man's time. Science on the other hand, science needed an army of educated men. Science was a place where men of above-average intelligence and education could find a foothold and push out the walls of knowledge. Science needed its rare geniuses, but it also needed its foot soldiers. My father had produced three of those foot soldiers. It was hard to convince him of anything else. I do not know everything that happened between my father and Martin after John's death. I was away at school, at Warden House then Charterhouse, but I believe there were a great many letters that passed back and forth between them. 'Your father has had another letter from Martin,' my mother's letters to me often read. She said no more but it meant that my father was greatly agitated and that my mother was writing me as a way of appearing busy and uninterruptible. She grew tired of the argument, though she never sided with anyone but my father, ever. Even after he was dead.

My long boarding school years were bookended by death. When I was twelve, I got word in Latin class that John had died. There were so many brothers of boys dying that they no longer took you out of class. You got a note, written on the deputy headmaster's yellow paper, and you were told that you could leave the room if you felt the need. Not even the most emotionally feeble among us would dream of admitting to such weakness, so I stayed in class while the teacher carried on and my classmates did anything but look in my direction. It wasn't tears you felt, not at first. It was more like being bathed in ethyl alcohol, which we used at home to anesthetize our insects. At night you cried, because everyone around you was crying, halls and halls of boys crying in the dark for their brothers. 'Tears are not endless and we have no more.' That is the line I like best of all those war poets.

Even still, it took a long time to feel much of anything again.

It was spring term of my last year at Charterhouse when I was called out of study hall and sent to the headmaster's office. He told me Martin had shot himself and was dead. My parents had given instructions that I was to finish the school term before coming home. Martin had killed himself on John's birthday beneath the statue of Anteros in Piccadilly Circus. There was an inquest, and a hearing, and his photograph on the front of the *Daily Mirror*. It was the most public suicide in English history. It must have been a great topic of conversation just beyond my earshot. To me, no one spoke a word.

I began my studies at Cambridge, where I took zoology, organic chemistry, botany, and physiology. That Christmas holiday I had planned to go to Spain with some chums, but the house fell through at the last minute and I ended up traveling the three miles to my parents' house, where my father had me join him in a study at the British Museum on the anomalous striped feathers of the red-legged partridge. Next term I began to suspect, as Martin had before me, that I was not made for science. And yet I *had* to be made for science; Martin had made it clear that any other path was not worth taking. The meaning of life is the quest to understand the structure and order of the natural world—that was the mantra I was raised on. To deviate from it was suicide. When an opportunity arose to go to the Galápagos, the Holy Grail, I leapt at it. That was where the spark would be rekindled, where I would become enlightened. But I found the work as tedious on a boat as it was in the Bird Room at the British Museum with my father. I came to see that the whole Darwinian story of the fat-beaked finches eating nuts and the thin-beaked finches eating grubs was bunk because they were all mixed in together eating caterpillars quite happily. The only discovery I made was that I love a warm humid climate. I had never felt so good in my skin. But I came home despondent about my future as a scientist. I knew that I could not spend my life in a laboratory.

I took a course in psychology. I joined the Cambridge Antiquarian Society and found myself on a train to Cheltenham for an archaeological dig. I had taken a fancy to a girl named Emma in the Society, and had hoped to maneuver it so I'd sit with her, but another fellow had had the same idea and a bit more foresight, so I was left on my own behind them. An older man, clearly a Cambridge don, took the seat beside me, and once I gave up my sulk about the girl, we began talking. He was curious about my trip to the Galápagos, not about the birds or the caterpillars but about the Ecuadorian mestizos. He asked a number of questions I didn't know how to answer but found intriguing and wished I'd thought to ask myself when I was there. He was A. C. Haddon, and this was my first conversation about a discipline he told me was called Anthropology. By the end of the ride, he'd invited me to do my Part II in Ethnology. Within a month, I'd switched over from the biological sciences. It was a bit terrifying, a bit of a free fall, to go from an extremely ordered and structured physical science to a nascent, barely twenty-year-old social science. Anthropology at that time was in transition, moving from the study of men dead and gone to the study of living people, and slowly letting go of the rigid belief that the natural and inevitable culmination of every society is the Western model.

I left for my first field trip the summer after I graduated. I could not get away fast enough. My father had died that winter (I'd been at his bedside; I'd had a chance to say goodbye, which made it easier) and my mother clung harder than usual to me. She became both unthinkably needy and cold-blooded. I do not know if she was trying to make up for the absence of my father or if his absence had unleashed a part of her personality that had been dormant during their long marriage. In either case, my mother was both anxious for my company and sickened by the man she imagined I was becoming. She thought anthropology a weak science, a false science, a phantasmagoria of words with no substance or purpose. She was so certain and uncompromising that even short visits were dangerous to my already wobbly convictions.

Initially I was supposed to find a tribe on the Sepik River of the Mandated Territory of New Guinea, an area which had yet to be penetrated by missionaries or industry. But when I arrived in Port Moresby I was told that the region wasn't safe. There had been a spate of headhunting raids. So I went to the island of New Britain where I studied the Baining, an impossible tribe who refused to tell me anything until I learned their language and when I had learned their language still refused to tell me. They would direct me to some person a half day's walk away and when I returned I would discover they'd held a ceremony in my absence. I could get nothing out of them and even after a year I hadn't figured out their genealogy because of a plethora of name taboos, which prevented them from ever saying aloud the names of certain relatives. But it must also be said that I had no idea what I was doing. For the first month I went around measuring their heads with calipers until someone asked me why and I had no answer apart from having been instructed to do so. I chucked the calipers away but never really understood what I was meant to be documenting instead. On my way home, I stopped in Sydney for a few months. Haddon was teaching at the university and he took me on as his assistant for his ethnography classes. In my spare time I worked on a monograph about the Baining. After he read it, Haddon claimed I was the first person to ever admit to having limitations as an anthropologist, to not understanding the natives when they conversed among themselves, to not having witnessed the full-blown version of a ceremony, to being duped and tricked and mocked. He was taken by my candor, but for me to have pretended otherwise would have been chicanery, like poor Kammerer injecting India ink into the feet of his midwife frogs to prove Lamarck's inheritance theory that characteristics acquired after birth can be passed on. At the end of the semester, I took a brief trip up the Sepik with my students to see a tribe or two, just to see what I had missed by not going there initially. I was quite taken with the Kiona, if only because when I asked a question through a translator, they answered it. We stayed four nights, and a week later I returned to England.

I'd been gone three years. I thought that might be enough travel for a while, but the combination of the winter gloom, my mother's restless bullying, and the stale cerebral self-conscious wit that bubbled like a frothy mold in every corner of Cambridge drove me to return to the Kiona as fast as I could manage.

5

My village of Nengai lay forty river miles west of Angoram. As the crow flies it would have been half that, but the Sepik, the longest river in New Guinea, is flamboyantly serpentine, the Amazon of the South Pacific, with a tendency to meander to such extremes that it has created, I learned a decade later under much different circumstances, over fifteen thousand oxbow lakes, places where the loops bent around so far they broke off. But when you are in a dugout canoe at night, even if it is motorized, you are not cognizant of the inefficient zig and zag of your route. You simply feel the river bend one way and then eventually another. You get used to the bugs in your eyes and mouth and the shiny rucked bulges of crocs and the thrash and bustle of thousands of nocturnal creatures gorging themselves while their predators sleep. You do not feel the extra, unnecessary twenty miles. If anything, you wish the trip were longer.

The thin moon gave the river a thin silver skin. As I had hoped, Nell nestled in among their bags and looked comfortable. I felt relieved when her eyes shut, as if she were my own croupy child who needed rest, and I puzzled over this feeling as Fen and I talked. We spoke not about our work but about Cambridge, where he'd been for a year while I was off with the Baining, and about Sydney, where we'd first met. We talked about football and Prime Minister MacDonald and India. The last I had heard, Gandhi had begun another hunger strike, but neither of us knew how it had ended. History hung suspended for months. I took solace in the not knowing.

After an hour or so of almost complete darkness on both banks, we came round a bend and saw fires and the flashes of festooned bodies all along a beach on the southern shore. It was the Olimbi village of Kamindimimbut, in the midst of a celebration. The smell of roasted boar reached us, and the hard drumming thudded in our chests.

It's hard to believe, as I write this account, that the next World War was only six years away from that night, or that in nine years the Japanese would take control of the Sepik and the whole of the New Guinea Territory from the Australians, or that I would let the United States government shake me down for every bit of knowledge I had about the area. Would Fen or Nell have done the same? Anthropological contribution, they called it in the OSS. A generous epithet for scientific prostitution.

I led a rescue operation up the Sepik to this village at the end of '42, and afterward every man, woman, and child of Kamindimimbut was killed by the Japanese when they learned a few Olimbi men had helped us find the three captured American agents being held nearby. Over three hundred people slaughtered solely because I knew which cluster of raised houses, which strip of sand, was theirs.

'What do you do about women then, Bankson?' Fen said quite out of the blue, after we'd passed Kamindimimbut.

I laughed. 'That's a bit personal for our first canoe trip, isn't it?'

'Just wondering if you've gone Malinowski's route. Say-ers visited the Trobriands last year and said there were quite a number of suspiciously tan-colored adolescents walking about.'

'Do you believe it?'

'Have you seen the man in action? Nell and I picked him up at the station in New York and the only thing he said to me was "I need a martini in my hand and a girl in my bed." Seriously, mate, it's rough alone. I don't think I could do it again.'

'I'll take a partner of some sort or other next time. More efficient, too, by half.'

'Not sure I'd go that far.' His spent cigarette made a brief orange arc into the river. I slowed for him to light another, then sped up again.

Sometimes at night it seemed to me that my boat was not being pushed by the engine but that boat and engine both were being pulled by the river itself, the ripples of wake just a design, like a stage set moving along with us.

'Sometimes I wish I'd gone to sea,' I said, perhaps simply for the luxury of being able to speak a passing thought aloud to someone who would understand what I meant.

'Do you? Why's that?'

'I think I'm better on water than land. Better in my skin, as the French say.'

'The ship captains I've met are tossers.'

'It would be nice to do a job that wasn't a big invisible knot to untangle, wouldn't it?'

He didn't answer, but I wasn't bothered. I was flattered that we'd gotten to this stage already, that our minds could wander without apology. We passed through a long swath of fireflies, thousands of them flashing all around us, and it felt like soaring through stars.

The dark shapes on land became increasingly familiar: the tall narrow blackboard tree I called Big Ben, the jut of blueschist rock, the high mud bank of the most western Kiona hamlet. I must have slowed for Fen said, 'Are we nearly there?'

'Mile or two more.'

'Nell,' he said in a regular voice, not so much a question as a test. Satisfied she was still asleep he leaned over and said to me quietly, 'Do the Kiona have a sacred object, removed from the village, something that they feed and protect?'

He'd already asked me many questions along these lines in Angoram. 'They have sacred objects, certainly—instruments and masks and skulls of old warriors.'

'That are kept in ceremonial houses?'

'Yes.'

'I mean something bigger. Kept apart. Something they might not have told you about, but you sense exists.'

He was suggesting that after nearly two years they were withholding some vital aspect of their society from me. I assured him that I had been shown every totemic object in their possession.

'They told me theirs was a descendant of a Kiona one.'

'The Mumbanyo told you this? About what?'

'Do me a favor and ask them again. About a flute. One that's sometimes kept in isolation and has to be fed.'

'Fed?'

'Could you ask while I'm there? Your informant might not tell you the truth, but at least I'll have a look at his reaction.'

'Did you see it?' I asked.

'I only found out about it a few days before we left.'

'And you saw it?'

'They sort of presented it to me.'

'As a gift?'

'Yes, I think so. As a gift. But then this other clan—there were two rivalrous clans in our village—took it back before I got a full look at the thing. I wanted to convince Nell to stay longer, but there is no rerouting her once she puts her mind to something.'

'Why did she want to leave?'

'Who knows. They didn't fit her thesis statement. And she calls the shots. We're on her grant money. Will you ask your man for me? About a sacred flute?'

'I've already shook them down hundreds of times about such things, but all right.'

'Thanks, mate. Just to see his face, really. See what it reveals.'

My beach appeared around the bend.

'Do you still have the butterfly net?' he said.

'What?'

'Haddon gave it to you in Sydney. Remember? Made me jealous.'

But I had no recollection of it.

I cut the engine and paddled in so as not to wake the village.

This time Fen shook her. 'Nell. We're here. We've reached the famous Kiona.'

'Hush. Let's not wake them,' she whispered. 'Lest we get shot by the arrows of the Great Warriors of the Sepik.'

'Princes,' Fen said. 'Princes of the Sepik.'

My house stood apart from the rest, and hadn't been lived in for many years. It was built around a rainbow gum tree, which came up through the floor and went out the roof. Many Kiona had come to believe it was a spirit tree, a place where their dead relatives gathered and made their plans, and some kept their distance, making a wide curve around my house when they passed by. They had offered to build me a house closer to the center of the village, but I had heard stories of anthropologists waiting months for their houses to be finished and I had been eager to settle in. I worried that Nell would have difficulty with my ladder, which was steep and nothing more than a wide pole with shallow notches for steps, but she climbed up, torch in hand, with ease. She didn't notice the tree until she was inside and the flame lit the room. I heard her let out a big American 'Wow.'

Fen and I hauled up their duffels, and I lit my three oil lamps to make the place seem more spacious. The gum tree took up a good bit of room. Nell stroked it. Its bark had shed and the trunk was smooth and streaked with orange and bright green and indigo. It wouldn't have been the first rainbow gum she'd encountered, but it was a striking specimen. She ran her palm down a swath of blue. I had the odd feeling that they were communicating, as if I had just introduced her to an old friend and they were already getting on well. For the truth is I had stroked that tree many a time, spoken to it, sobbed against it. I busied myself, gathering my medicines and looking for my whiskey, because I was tired and a bit raw from the long night and long ride, and I could not be certain I wouldn't well up right then if she asked me a single question about my tree.

'Ah, just what I was dreaming of,' Fen said when he peered into the tin cup I handed him.

The two of us sat on the little sofas I'd made from bark cloth and kapok fiber while Nell wandered about. My body felt like it was still skimming across the water.

'Don't snoop, Nellie,' he called over his shoulder. And then to me: 'Americans make such good anthropologists because they're so bloody rude.'

'You're admitting I'm a good anthropologist?' she said from my workroom.

'I'm saying you're a nosy parker.'

She was bent over my desk, not touching anything, but looking closely. I could see there was a sheet of paper in the typewriter, but I couldn't remember what it said.

'Those wounds of hers need treating.'

Fen nodded.

'I've never seen how anyone else works in the field,' she said.

'I guess I don't count,' Fen said.

'Is that mango leaves? You have a question here about mango leaves.'

'And now she's going to solve your problem, having been here a full five minutes.'

I feigned confusion and joined her in the workroom.

She was looking at the great mess of notebooks and loose papers and carbons.

'This makes me miss the work.'

'It's only been a few days, hasn't it?'

'I never settled in with the Mumbanyo like this.' She looked at my clutter of papers as if it had value, as if she were certain something substantial would come out of it somehow.

I saw the note she'd been referring to.

mgo lvs again on grv. ??

I explained that I'd been to the burial of a boy in another Kiona hamlet and mango leaves were carefully placed over the grave.

'You'd seen the pattern before?'

'No, a different leaf pattern each time. But I can't find the pattern to the patterns.'

'Age, sex, social status, mode of death, shape of the moon, position of the stars, birth order, role in family.' She stopped to take a breath. She looked like she had about forty-five other ideas for me.

'No. They keep telling me there is no pattern.'

'Perhaps there isn't.'

'The same old woman quietly gives the instructions.'

'And when you ask her directly?'

'Leave it alone, Nell,' Fen said from the sofa. 'He's been here twice the time you have, for Christ's sake.'

'It's all right. I could use some help. She's the one woman in the area who won't speak to me.'

'Not even indirectly, through a relative?'

'A white man killed her son.'

43

'Do you know the circumstances?'

'There had been some fighting downriver and the kiaps came in for a roundup. They calaboosed half the village. This young man had been visiting his cousin—nothing to do with the fight—resisted arrest, and died from a blow to the head.'

'Have you made amends?'

'What?'

'Have you made offerings to this woman for the mistake of your kin?'

'Those pigs are hardly my kin.'

'To that woman they are. They don't think there are more than twelve of us in the whole world.'

'I've given her salt and matches and tried to charm her in every way I can think of.'

'Is there a formal amends ritual?'

'I don't know.'

She looked exasperated with me. 'You can't afford to have someone so set against you. Everyone will know it and measure their response to you against it. She's skewing all your results.'

Fen cackled behind us. 'Didn't take you long this time. I think that might be a record. Shall we make a pyre of all his notes?'

All her face could muster was a pale peach flush. 'I'm sorry, I—' She put her hand out halfway to me.

'I'm sure you're right. I should find out how to make amends.'

She didn't seem to believe my tone of voice or the expression on my face, and apologized again. But I wasn't put out by what she'd said. Quite the opposite. I was eager, desperate

44

for more. Ideas, suggestions, criticism of my approach. Fen might have had too much of it, but I had had too little.

'Let's see about treating those battle wounds.'

I went to the back of the house to fetch the medicines I'd collected.

I heard Fen say, 'Well, you gave him a right sheep-dipping, didn't you?'

I didn't hear Nell respond. When I came back, she was sitting beside him and her face had returned to its eerie yellow.

Fen made no move to do it himself, so I asked for her left hand first, the one with the gash across the palm. I couldn't understand how they'd been so cavalier about these cuts. Sepsis was one of the greatest risks in the field.

Fen must have seen something in my face. 'Our medicine disappears in a week,' he said. 'Every time we get a shipment Nell uses it up on the scrapes and sores of all her kiddies.'

I doused the cut in iodine, swabbed it with boracic ointment, and wrapped it in a cotton bandage. Her hand at first was weightless in mine but soon it gave in and grew heavy.

I confess, I worked slowly. After the hand I addressed the lesions, two on her arm, one on her neck, and—she rolled up her pant leg—another on her right shin. They seemed to me to be small tropical ulcers, not yaws. I suspected there were more, but I could hardly ask her to remove her clothing. I gave her aspirin for her fever. Beside her Fen watched until his eyes closed.

'You must let me apologize for what I said earlier,' she said, 'about the leaves.'

'Formal amends would require an oath that you two don't run off to the Aborigines.'

She raised her bandaged hand. 'I swear.'

'Now, tell me what happened with the Mumbanyo. Unless you want to sleep.'

'I got my rest in the canoe. Thank you for the tending. Everything feels better.' She took her first sip of whiskey. 'Do you know of them, the Mumbanyo?'

'Never heard of them.'

'Fen will give you a very different account than mine.' Her wounds glistened with the ointment I had put on them.

'Give me yours.'

She seemed daunted by the question, as if I'd asked her to write a monograph about them on the spot. Just when I thought she'd say she was too tired, she launched in. They were an affluent tribe, unlike the Anapa, who struggled to get enough to eat each day. The Mumbanyo's tributary was full of fish, and they grew all the tobacco in the area. They were flush with food and shell money. But they were full of fear and aggression, bordering on paranoia, and terrified the region into submission with their impulsive threats.

'I've never had an aversion to a people before. Almost a physical repulsion. I'm not a neophyte to the region. I've seen deaths, sacrifices, scarrings that end badly. I'm not—' She looked at me wildly. 'They kill their firstborn. They kill all their twins. Not in a ritual, not with emotion and ceremony. They just toss them in the river. Toss them in the bush. And the children they keep, they barely tend to. They carry them under their arm like a newspaper or plunk them in stiff baskets and close the lid, and when the baby cries they scratch the basket. That's their most tender gesture, the scratching on the outside of the basket. When the girls are seven or eight, their fathers start to have sex with them. No surprise they grow up distrustful, vindictive, and murderous. And Fen—'

'He was intrigued?'

'Yes. Enamored. Utterly compelled. I had to get him out of there.' She tried to laugh. 'They kept telling us they were on their best behavior for us, but that it wouldn't last forever. They were blaming everything that went wrong on the lack of bloodshed. We left seven months early. Maybe you noticed—there's sort of a stench of failure about us.'

'I hadn't caught that, no.' I would have liked to tell her about my own sense of failure, but it felt too vast to explain. Instead I looked at her shoes, leather schoolgirl lace-ups nearly as worn out as my own. I couldn't be sure she had all her toes in there. Toes were the first things to get eaten away by those tropical ulcers.

'You have a letter to your mother in the typewriter,' she said.

'I often do. Dear Mum, leave me alone. Love, Andrew.'

'Andrew.'

'Yes.'

'No one ever calls you that.'

'No one. Except my mum.' I felt her waiting for more. 'She would like me to be in a laboratory in Cambridge. Threatens to cut me off in every letter. And I can't do this work without her support. We don't have the kind of grants you have in America. Nor have I written a best-selling book, or any book for that matter.' She'd ask next about the rest of the family, so I thought I should head her off. 'Everyone else is dead so she seems to have a great deal of energy for me.'

'Who is everybody else?'

'My father and brothers.'

'How?'

There was an American anthropologist for you. No delicate changing of the subject, no *You have my deepest condolences* or even *How ghastly for you*, but just a no-nonsense, straight-on *How the heck did that happen?*

'John in the war. Martin in an accident six years later. And my father of heart failure, most likely due to the sad fact that runty old me was all that was left of his legacy.'

'Hardly runty.'

'Runty in the brain. My brothers were geniuses in their own ways.'

'Everyone becomes a genius when they die young. What were they smart at?'

I told her about John and his boots and pail, the rare moth, the fossils in the trenches. And about Martin. 'My father thought it showed inordinate hubris for Martin to try and write a poem.'

'Fen told me your father coined the word *genetics*.'

'He didn't mean to. He wanted to teach a course on Mendel and what was then called gene plasma. He felt it needed a more dignified word than plasma.'

'Did he want you to continue where he left off?'

'He wasn't capable of imagining anything else for us. It was all that mattered to him. He believed it was our duty.'

'When did he die?'

'Nine years this winter.'

'So he knew you'd transgressed.'

'He knew I was reading ethnography with Haddon.'

'He thought it was a soft science?'

'It wasn't science at all. Not to him.' I could hear my father clearly. *Pure nonsense.*

'And your mother is of the same persuasion?'

'Stalin to his Lenin. I am nearly thirty but entirely in her thrall. My father left it that she hold the purse strings.'

'Well, you've managed to build your jail cell at a good distance from her.'

I felt I should encourage her to sleep. You need rest, I should have said, but did not. 'It wasn't an accident. With Martin. He killed himself.'

'Why?'

'He was in love with a girl and she didn't want him. He'd gone to her flat with a love poem he'd written and she wouldn't read it. So he went and stood under the statue of Anteros in Piccadilly Circus and shot himself. I have the poem. It's not his best. But the bloodstains give it a little dignity.'

'How old were you?'

'Eighteen.'

'I thought it was Eros in Piccadilly.' She plucked at a pencil on my desk. For a second I thought she was going to start taking notes.

'Many people do. But it's his twin brother, the avenger of unrequited love. Poetic to the last.'

Most women like to fuss around a wound of your past, pick at the thin scab, comfort you after they'd made it sting. Not Nell.

'Do you have a favorite part of all this?' she asked.

'All what?' I said.

'This work.'

Favorite part? There was little at this point that didn't make me want to run with my stones straight back into the river. I shook my head. 'You first.'

She looked surprised, as if she hadn't expected the question to come back at her. She narrowed her grey eyes. 'It's that moment about two months in, when you think you've finally got a handle on the place. Suddenly it feels within your grasp. It's a delusion—you've only been there eight weeks—and it's followed by the complete despair of ever understanding anything. But at that moment the place feels entirely yours. It's the briefest, purest euphoria.'

'Bloody hell.' I laughed.

'You don't get that?'

'Christ, no. A good day for me is when no little boy steals my underwear, pokes it through with sticks, and brings it back stuffed with rats.'

I asked her if she believed you could ever truly understand another culture. I told her the longer I stayed, the more asinine the attempt seemed, and that what I'd become more interested in is how we believed we could be objective in any way at all, we who each came in with our own personal definitions of kindness, strength, masculinity, femininity, God, civilization, right and wrong.

She told me I sounded as skeptical as my father. She said no one had more than one perspective, not even in his so-called hard sciences. We're always, in everything we do in this world, she said, limited by subjectivity. But our perspective can have an enormous wingspan, if we give it the freedom to unfurl. Look at Malinowski, she said. Look at Boas. They defined their cultures as they saw them, as *they* understood the natives' point of view. The key is, she said, to disengage yourself from all your ideas about what is "natural."

'Even if I manage that, the next person who comes here will tell a different story about the Kiona.'

'No doubt.'

'Then what is the *point*?' I said.

'This is no different from the laboratory. What's the *point* of anyone's search for answers? The truth you find will always be replaced by someone else's. Someday even Darwin will look like a quaint Ptolemy who saw what he could see but no more.'

'I'm a little mired at the moment.' I wiped my face with my hands, healthy hands—my body thrived in the tropics; it was my mind that threatened to give out on me. 'You don't struggle with these questions?'

'No. But I've always thought my opinion was the right one. It's a small flaw I have.'

'An American flaw.'

'Maybe. But Fen has it, too.'

'A flaw of the colonies then. Is that why you got into this line of work, so you could have your say and people would have to travel thousands of miles and write their own book if they wanted to refute you?'

She smiled broadly.

'What is it?' I asked.

'This is the second time tonight I've remembered this tiny thing I haven't thought of for years.'

'What's that?'

'My first report card. I wasn't sent to school until I was nine, and my teacher's comment at the end of the first term was: "Elinor has an overenthusiasm for her own ideas and a voluble dearth of enthusiasm for those of others, most especially her teacher's."'

I laughed. 'When was the first time you thought of it?'

'When we first arrived, and I was poking around your desk. All your notes and papers and books—I felt a rush of ideas, which is something I haven't felt in a while. I thought maybe it was gone for good. You look like you don't believe me.'

'I believe you. I'm just terrified by what overenthusiasm might look like. If what I am seeing now is underenthusiasm.'

'If you're anything like Fen, you won't like it much.'

I guessed I wasn't anything like Fen.

She looked at her husband, who was in a deep concentrated sleep beside her, lips pursed and brow wrinkled, as if resisting being fed.

'How did the two of you meet?'

'On a ship. After my first field trip.'

'Shipboard romance.' It came out almost as a question, as if I were asking if it had been too hasty, and I quickly added, weakly, 'The best kind.'

'Yes. It was very sudden. I was coming back from the Solomons. A group of Canadian tourists on the boat was making a great fuss about me having studied the natives unchaperoned and I was full of stories for them and Fen sort of skulked around in the shadows for a few days. I didn't know who he was—nobody did—but he was the only man my age and he wouldn't dance with me. And then out of the blue, he came up to me at breakfast and asked what I had dreamed the night before. I learned he'd been studying the dreams of a tribe called the Dobu, and he was heading to London to teach. Honestly it was such a surprise, that this burly black-haired Aussie was an anthropologist like me. We were both coming back from our first field trips and we had a lot to talk about. He was so full of energy and humor. The Dobu are all sorcerers so Fen kept putting spells and hexes on people, and we'd hide and see if they worked. We were like little kids, giddy at having found a friend among all these stuffy grown-ups. And Fen loves to live with an us-against-the-world mentality that is very alluring at first. All the other passengers fell away. We talked and laughed our way to Marseille. Two and a half months. You really think you know a person after that kind of time together.' She was looking somewhere over my left shoulder. She didn't seem to notice she'd stopped talking. I wondered if she'd fallen asleep with her eyes open. Then they drifted back. 'He went on to London to teach for a semester. I went home to New York to write my book. We were married a year later and came here.'

She was exhausted.

'Let me sort out a bed for you,' I said, getting up.

I went into the small mosquito room I slept in. The sheets on the mat hadn't been changed for weeks and my clothes were strewn everywhere. I shoved everything in the crate I used for a bedside table and spread clean sheets on the mat in the best version of a real bed that I could manage. I had a nice pillow, one from my mother's house, but the humidity had stuck the feathers together so it felt more like clay than down.

I heard laughing behind me. She was standing on the other side of the netting, observing my attempts to fluff it up.

'Please don't worry about that. But point me in the direction of the latrine, if you have one.'

I took her out to it. You had to have them built a good distance from the house in the tropics. I'd learned that the hard way with the Baining. The sky had lightened and we didn't need a torch. I wasn't sure what state the latrine would be in, having never expected a woman to use it, and I planned to have a look before I let her in, but she reached it first and jumped in before I could stop her.

Now I was in a predicament. I felt I should stay close by, in case there was a snake or a bat, both of which I had encountered in that small space before, as well as a flying fox and an enchanting red and gold bird Teket thought I had imagined. But I also felt one needed privacy to perform one's duties. Before I could decide the proper distance at which to stand, her water began to flow at an astonishing rate and kept on for a great while. Then she was out the door and back on the path with me, limping along but with a new burst of energy.

When we returned, Fen had shifted over to one side and was releasing his breath in great suspended puffs, like a surfacing whale. It felt to me like a terribly intimate noise and I wished I'd gotten him to the bedroom before he'd entered such a deep sleep. I thought Nell would go to bed then, but she followed me to the back of the house, where I was planning to make a cup of tea and think of where I could take them to find a decent tribe.

She asked me what the last piece of the puzzle here was, and I told her about a Kiona ceremony called Wai I'd seen only once, when I first arrived, and my nascent thoughts about the transvestitism involved. She asked if I'd ever tried my ideas out on them.

I laughed. '"I say, Nmebito, did you know that by embracing your feminine side that night you have provided an equilibrium for this community that the overdeveloped masculine aggression of your culture often threatens?" Is that what you mean?'

'Maybe something more like: Do you think men becoming women and women becoming men brings joy and peace?'

'But they're not reflective in that way.'

'Of course they are. They reflect on when they fished the day before—what it brought them, where they might choose to go the next day. They reflect on their children, their spouses, their siblings, their debts, their promises.'

'But I see no evidence of the Kiona analyzing their own rituals in search of meaning,' I said.

'I'm sure some do. It's just that they've been born into a culture that makes no place for it, so the impulse weakens, like an unused muscle. You need to help them exercise it.'

'Is this what you do?'

'Not all in one day, but yes. The meaning is inside *them*, not inside you. You just have to pull it out.'

'You're assuming analytical abilities that I'm not sure they possess.'

'They are human, with fully functioning human minds. If I didn't believe they shared my humanity entirely, I wouldn't be here.' She had real color in her cheeks now. 'I'm not interested in zoology.'

Observe observe observe, I'd always been instructed. Nothing about sharing your findings or eliciting analysis from the subjects themselves. 'Wouldn't this approach create a self-consciousness in the subject that would then alter the results?'

'I think observing without sharing the observations creates an atmosphere of extreme artificiality. They don't understand why you're there. If you are open with them, everybody becomes more relaxed and honest.'

She was looking like a cuscus again, her face so alert and those wide grey eyes slightly unfocused. 'Can we sit and drink that tea?'

When we did she said, 'Freud said that primitives are like Western children. I don't believe that for a second, but most anthropologists don't blink an eye at it, so we'll let it stand for the sake of my argument, which is: Every child seeks meaning. When I was four I remember asking my quite pregnant mother: What's the point of all this? Of all what? she asked. Of all this *life*. I remember how she looked at me and I felt like I'd said something very bad. She came and sat beside me at the table and told me I'd just asked a very big question, and that I wouldn't be able to answer it until I was an old, old woman. But she was wrong. Because she had that baby, and when she brought her home I knew I'd found the point. Her name was Katie but everyone called her Nell's Baby. She was my baby. I did everything for her: fed her, changed her, dressed her, put her to sleep. And then when she was nine months old, she got sick. I was sent to my aunt's in New Jersey and when I came back she was gone. They didn't even let me say goodbye. I couldn't even touch her or hold her. She was gone like a rug or a chair. I feel like I got most of life's lessons before I turned six. For me, other people are the point, but other people can disappear. I guess I don't have to tell you that.'

'The Kiona give everyone a sacred name, a secret spirit name to use in the world beyond this one. I gave John and Martin new names and I find it helps a bit. Brings them closer somehow.' My heart was suddenly beating hard. 'Was Katie your only sibling?'

'No. My mother had a boy two years later. Michael. But I couldn't go near him. I said mean things about him. I think that's why they finally sent me to school. To get me out of poor Michael's hair.'

'And what do you make of him now?'

'Not much. He's quite angry with me at the moment, because I haven't changed my name to Fen's, and that has been reported in the papers in several cities.'

I'd heard that, too, somewhere.

'Were you close to your brothers?' she asked.

'Yes, but I didn't know it until they died.' I felt my throat tighten a bit, but I pushed the words through. 'When John died I was twelve and I thought, if only it had been Martin. I thought I could have handled Martin better because he was so much more familiar and irritating to me. John was like a beloved uncle who came home and took me frog hunting and bought me jelly buttons. Martin taunted and mimicked me. And then six years after John, Martin did die and I felt like—' And then my throat closed entirely and I couldn't force it open. She stared at me and nodded into the silence between us, as if I were still talking and making perfect sense.

6

There is no privacy through a mosquito net. Next morning, as Fen and I sat at my table with a map of the river we'd sketched out together, Nell rolled onto her back and slowly sat up. She laid her cheek on a knee and didn't move again for a long time.

'I think she's worse today,' I said. A malarial fever came on hard with a headache that felt like someone was taking an axe to the base of your skull.

'Nellie. Up and at 'em,' he said without turning. 'We've got tribes to meet today.' He said to me, quietly, 'The trick is to outrun it. Stop moving and you're buggered.'

'In my experience it doesn't always give you that option.' When my fever came on, my body felt filled with lead, and I was lucky if I could reach a chamber pot. I fetched the medicine box.

'I'm going to the loo,' he said to her through the netting. 'Please don't slow us down.'

If she responded I couldn't hear it. Her cheek remained pressed to her knee. Fen disappeared down the pole.

She was not in any state of undress—she wore the same shirt and pants from the night before—yet I felt reluctant to greet her. I wanted to give her the illusion of privacy. I busied myself with turning some yams in the ash fire and doing the washing up at the back of the house, though there were only

58

two plates and two cups and they needed little more than a wipe-down.

'Did you sleep at all?'

I swung round. She was seated at the table.

'A bit,' I said.

'Liar.'

Her cheeks were flushed in wide circles like a doll's, but her lips were colorless, her eyes glazed yellow. I tapped out four aspirin into my hand. 'Too many?'

She leaned in from across the table, peering closely at the pills. 'Perfect.'

'You need specs.'

'I stepped on them a few months ago.'

'Bankson! A fellow's here,' Fen called from below. 'I can't make out what he wants.'

'I'll be right down.' I brought Nell water for her pills and went to the smaller trunk in my office. I swept my hand back and forth across its gritty bottom until I felt the small case in a corner. I hadn't opened it since my mother gave it to me before I sailed.

'I don't know how they'll do,' I said, handing it to her.

She snapped it open. They had a simple wire frame, thinner than I remembered. Pewter-colored. A near perfect match to her eyes.

'Don't you need them?'

'They were Martin's.' A policeman had come to the door with them several months after his death. They'd been freshly polished, and a tag on a string had been knotted to the bridge.

She seemed to understand all that, and lifted them tenderly from their dingy case to put them on.

'Oh,' she said, moving toward the window. 'They're out on the water with their nets.' She turned back around to look at me, still holding the frames to her face with two hands as if they would not stay there by themselves. 'And you could stand a shave, Mr. Bankson.'

'They work then?'

'I think I may be more myopic than Martin, but we're close.'

It was lovely, hearing Martin spoken of in the present tense. 'Keep them.'

'I couldn't.'

'I've plenty of his things.' It wasn't true. There was a sweater or two in my mother's closet, but that was all. My father had ordered the servants to give it all to a charity shop as soon as his trunks had arrived from London. 'Happy Christmas,' I said.

She smiled, remembering this. 'I'll take good care of them.'

They were big for her small marsupial face, but suited her somehow. You get hounded daily in the field for your possessions, and it felt good to give something away that hadn't been asked for.

'Bankson, help me out here!'

I went down to Fen, who was face-to-face with one of my informants, Ragwa, who was meant to take me to a naming ceremony in his sister's hamlet this afternoon. Ragwa had taken up the Kiona intimidation position, arms bowed and chin stretched out over his feet, and Fen had done nothing but encourage it by taking up his own, either in mockery or for real, I couldn't tell which.

60

'Ask him about the sacred object,' Fen whispered.

But Ragwa cut me off and said his wife had gone into labor and he couldn't accompany me today. After that he rushed off.

"They all like that?'

'He's worried about his wife. The baby's early.' A few weeks ago Ragwa had grabbed my hand and pressed it to his wife's belly. I felt the baby roll beneath her taut skin. I had never felt that before, never known, honestly, that such a thing happened. It echoed against my palm for a long time after. It was like putting my hand to the surface of the ocean and being able to feel a fish beneath. Ragwa had laughed and laughed at the expression on my face.

'Can I help with the birth?' Nell was standing in the doorway.

'I thought we were leaving,' Fen said, not noticing her spectacles.

'But if the baby's premature.'

'They've been having babies for a long time without you, Nell.'

'I have some experience,' she said to me.

'It's very kind. But there's a taboo on childless women witnessing a birth.'

She nodded. 'The Anapa were the same,' she said, but her voice had lost some strength, and I felt I'd said the wrong thing.

'And we do need to see if we can find something, Nellie,' Fen said more gently than I'd ever heard him speak.

I gave them a tour of the village, and an hour later we set off to the Ngoni. I had made a case for this tribe: They were skilled warriors, which would appeal to Fen, and renowned healers, which I thought might interest—and help—Nell. But the real reason I'd chosen the Ngoni was that they were less than an hour's boat ride from my village.

We were hungry as soon as we got on the water. I had packed enough food for several days if need be. We ate with our hands, scooping our fingers into still warm baked yams and the cool flesh of a jackfruit. I made sure the food made equal rounds up to Nell in the bow, and that she was taking it. After she ate she seemed to revive a bit, looking ahead and turning back toward me, her hair rising behind her, with questions about adzes, kina shells, and creation stories.

The Ngoni were just beyond the sandbar I always had to watch out for in the dark. The hamlet's houses were arranged in groups of three, set back fifteen feet from the steep riverbank and, like all houses in the region, raised on piles to keep out vermin and the river when it rose.

'No beach?' Nell said.

I hadn't thought about that. It was true. The land dropped into the water abruptly.

'It's a bit gloomy, isn't it?' Fen said. 'Not much sunlight.'

At the sound of the approaching engine, a few men had gathered at the edge of their land.

'Let's keep going, Bankson,' Nell said. 'Let's not stop here.'

Next were the Yarapat, but Fen thought the houses hung too low to the ground. I tried to point out the rise in the land—the Yarapat were set on a high hill—but he'd been flooded once in the Admiralty Islands, so we passed them by as well.

They didn't like the looks of the next village, either.

'Weak art,' Nell said.

'What?'

'That face,' she said, meaning the enormous mask that hung over the entryway of the ceremonial house we could see from the water. 'It's crude. Not like what I've seen elsewhere.'

'We need art, Bankson,' Fen bellowed poshly from his seat in front of me. 'We need art and theatre and the *ballet*, if it's not too much bother.'

'Do you want to stop here?' Nell asked him.

'No.'

We were now four hours away from Nengai, and the sun was dropping fast, the way it does near the equator. We hadn't even got out of the boat yet. I knew of one more tribe, the Wokup, before my familiarity with the river in this direction ran out. The Wokup had a beach, tall houses, and good art.

When we reached them, I gunned the boat directly at the center of the beach, determined that I would not stop for any reservation they could cook up. Though I was concentrating on the shore beyond her, I felt Nell imitating the stubborn clench in my face. But I thought she'd been a fusspot about the other tribes and could find no humor in it.

No one came down to greet us at the sound of the boat. Then I heard a call, not a drum, and there were flickers of quick movement, a child's shriek, then nothing.

I had met a few Wokup. They were not ignorant of whites—no one on this part of the river was by now. Most tribes had a story of someone being put in jail or lured away by recruiters—blackbirders, they were called then—to the mines. I pulled the canoe up onto the shore and we sat in it, waiting, not wanting to cause more distress. A second call went up and a minute later three men came down to greet us. I could not see their backs, but the raised scars on their arms were longer, more like strands of hair or rays of the sun, than the crocodile hide designs of the Kiona. Save a few armbands, they were naked and took their positions in the sand. They knew, even if they had never seen it themselves, that whites had powers—steel blades, rifles, pistols, dynamite—that they did not possess. They knew this power could come on suddenly, with no warning. But we are not afraid, they said with their spread legs, arched backs, and hard gazes.

The one in the middle recognized me from trading at Timbunke and spoke to me in Kiona fragments. From what I could piece together, their village was expecting a raid from a swamp tribe. Swamp tribes were low in the pecking order of the Sepik, weak and impoverished, but they were unpredictable. I explained that my friends were interested in living with them and understanding their ways, that they had many gifts—but he waved me off before I could finish. It was a bad time, he said many times. There was the raid, and there was something else I couldn't understand. A bad time. We were welcome to spend the night—he could not guarantee us a safe trip home in the dark if their enemies were en route—but we would have to leave in the morning.

'I don't know how much of this is true,' I said to Nell and Fen after I translated everything the chief had said. 'He could be waiting for some incentives.'

'Tell him we can supply him with ten years' worth of salt and matches for the whole tribe,' Fen said.

'We can't lie.'

'We still have loads of the stuff in Port Moresby.'

To verify this with Nell would insult him, yet it seemed impossible that after a year and a half they would still have that much to offer.

'We are not light travelers,' she said.

I began to communicate this to the chief but he raised his hand before I could finish, insulted. He explained that they lacked nothing and needed nothing from us, but for our safety and the safety of his people, he would let us stay the night.

We followed the three Wokup up to the village center. A boy was sent up the ladder of a house and within minutes a mother and five children climbed down. Without looking at us they made their way to a house three doors away. The children let out small yelps once they were inside. The adults hushed them angrily.

The chief indicated that we were to go up. Fen went first with our bag, then reached down to help me with the engine. It was a small house. I suspected that it must be the second or third wife of the chief, whose house next door was much larger. We watched him climb up his ladder and disappear.

We were in near darkness. All the openings were covered with bark cloth dyed black. The village was silent. We could nearly hear the sweat coming out of our pores.

'Crikey. They could have bloody well offered us some food,' Fen said.

Nell hushed him.

He fished around in his duffel. I thought he was going to produce some extra tins he'd stashed away, but he pulled out a revolver.

I felt my blood rushing, stinging.

'Put it away, Fen,' Nell said. 'We won't need it.'

'They seem serious. Did you see all those spears?'

Nell didn't say anything.

'The spears leaning against the house on the other side of the chief. You didn't see them?' He seemed quite giddy with this fact. 'Sharp. Maybe poisoned."

'Fen. Stop it.' She was stern.

He slid the gun back in his bag. 'They aren't messing around.' He moved low and fast to the doorway and peered sideways through a crack in the bark cloth. 'I think we should sleep in rotations, Bankson.'

There wasn't going to be much sleeping, anyway. The house caught no breeze and the bugs were awful. We ate from our provisions, played a few hands of dummy bridge by the light of a candle, then chose our beds. The Wokup slept in covered hammocks, not in bags like the Kiona or on mats like the Baining. I took the one in the far corner. It looked to be about a foot and a half shorter than what I could fit into, so I told Fen I'd take the first shift. He motioned to the gun, but I left it in his duffel.

I rolled up the bark cloth a bit and sat in the doorway against a beam. A mist, torn in places, lay across the river now. Behind me Nell and Fen tried to get comfortable in their hammocks. 'It's like sleeping inside a teabag,' I heard him say. Nell laughed and said something I couldn't hear that made him laugh. It was the first time I had felt alone with them, and it hit me hard and low in the gut. They were here but they belonged to each other and they would go off again and leave me behind.

Outside the sounds of the jungle rose up. Croaks, thrashes, screeches. Whining, growling, splashing. Hums, thrums, and whirs. Every creature seemed on the move. On bad nights in Nengai I'd imagined they were all coming slowly for me.

I tried to focus on the immediate future, tomorrow, and not the great swath of time that stretched out perilously after that. I'd have to take them to Lake Tam. Another three hours upriver. Seven hours away from me. My visits, if I made them, would be planned and certainly less frequent. I'd have to stay the night, disrupt their routines. I was ashamed to feel such bald need for these near strangers, and as I sat there in the dark I trained my mind back to my work, though if there was a quicker way back to suicidal thoughts, I did not know it. But earlier in the day, I'd had another conversation with Nell about the Wai, and as we talked I had the idea that perhaps through this ceremony I could tell the story of the Kiona. I had hundreds of pages of notes, but I wasn't any closer to a full understanding of it. Once elaborate and in celebration of a boy's first homicide, the Wai ceremony was performed infrequently now, no longer to recognize a killing but in honor of any sort of young male's accomplishment: first fish caught, first boar speared, first canoe built. Many firsts in the past two years had passed unacknowledged, however, and though I was often promised another Wai soon, soon never seemed to come.

I shut my eyes and remembered the ceremony as I had witnessed it. It had been during my first month and I'd been sitting with the women—I was often put with the women in large gatherings, along with the children and the mentally ill. To my left was Tupani-Kwo, one of the oldest women of the village. I managed to ask her a few questions, but I hadn't understood many of her answers. It was chaotic. The father and uncles of the boy being celebrated came out first, in dirty tattered skirts and strings around their bellies like pregnant women wore. They hobbled along together as if they were sick or dying. The women came next, wearing male headdresses and necklaces made of homicidal ornaments and large orange penis gourds strapped around their genitals. They carried the men's lime boxes and pushed the notched lime sticks in and out to make a loud noise and to show off the swinging tassels which hung from the end of the sticks, each one representing a past murder. The women walked tall and proud, appearing to enjoy the role. The boy and a few of his friends ran to them with big walking sticks and the women put down their lime boxes, took the sticks, and beat the men until they ran away.

I crept quietly back to get my notebook and citronella candle. Fen and Nell were dark lumps, hanging in their hammocks. Back in my spot in the doorway, I wrote about my most recent conversation with Tupani-Kwo about that day. I was surprised by the energy I suddenly had for it. The thoughts came fast, and I caught them, stopping only once to sharpen my pencil with a penknife. I thought of Nell's euphoria and nearly laughed out loud. This little rush of words was the closest I'd come to any sort of elation in the field.

Behind me the stiff fibers of a hammock creaked and Nell came and sat beside me, her bare feet on the top rung of the ladder. She did have all ten toes.

'I can't sleep if someone else is working,' she said.

'Done.' I closed the notebook.

'No, please, continue. It's also soothing.'

'I was waiting for more words. I don't think they were coming.'

She laughed.

'What's funny?' I said.

'You keep reminding me of things.'

'Tell me.'

'It's just a story my father likes to repeat. I have no memory of it. He says at three or four I had a big tantrum and locked myself in my mother's closet. I tore down her dresses and kicked her shoes all around, and made a terrible amount of noise, then there was absolute silence for a long time. "Nellie?" my mother said. "Are you all right?" and apparently I said, "I've spit on your dresses and I've spit on your hats and now I'm waiting for more spit."'

I laughed. I could see her with a round red face and a wild thicket of hair.

'I promise that's the last Nell Stone childhood vignette I will bore you with.'

'Do you still amuse your parents?' It was something I couldn't imagine being able to do anymore.

She laughed. 'Not in the least.'

'Why not?'

'I wrote a book all about the sex lives of native children.'

'That is a bit less seemly than spitting on hats, isn't it?'

'A good bit less,' she said in my accent. She put on Martin's glasses. She'd been holding them in her hand. 'The reactions to this book have been out of proportion. I was glad to escape the country.'

'I'm sorry I haven't read it.'

'You have a pretty good excuse.'

'I should have had someone send it.'

'They haven't warmed to it in England,' she said. 'Now go get some sleep. I'll take this watch. Oh, look at the moon.'

It was the slightest paring, the rest of the unlit moon a faint aura behind it.

'"I saw the new moon, late yestereen, with the old moon in her arm,"' she said with a Scottish burr.

'"And I fear, I fear, my maister dear—"' I continued.

'"That we shall come to harm."'

'"They had na sail'd a league, a league,"' I said, thickening my own accent.

'"A league but barely three—"'

'"When the lift grew dark and the wind blew loud—"'

She joined me here, '"And gurly grew the sea."' I kept my eyes on the moon, but I heard the smile in her voice.

Americans could surprise you with the things they knew.

I'm not sure what we said after that, if it was a long time or a short time that went by before there was a snap and a thud behind us. We jumped up. Fen was on the ground in his hammock. I held the candle over him while Nell crouched down. His eyes were shut, and when she nudged him and asked him if he was all right, he said, 'It's always rough, this patch.' And then, 'Knock it with a shoe, yer git,' and rolled over.

'I think he's trying to open a bottle of beer.'

We had a good laugh and left him be. I made a little bed with my extra clothes in the corner below my hammock. I didn't think I'd actually sleep but I did, quite soundly, and they were packed up and waiting for me when I woke.

Nearly all the Wokup were on the beach to see us off. They yipped and hooted and the children flung themselves in the water.

'A lot stronger on goodbye than hello, aren't they?' Fen said.

'There never was a raid coming from the swamp,' I said.

'Probably not,' Nell said.

Fen asked to drive the boat so I slowed and we wobbily swapped places. He opened up the throttle and we were off—fast.

'Fen!' Nell screeched, but she was half laughing. She turned around to face us and her knees brushed my shins. 'I can't watch. Tell me when we're about to crash.' Her hair, no longer plaited, blew toward me. The fever and loose hair, dark brown with threads of copper and gold, had brought an illusion of great health to her face.

If the Tam weren't a good fit, they would go to Australia. This was my last chance to get it right. And I could tell she was skeptical. But Teket had been many times to the Tam to visit his cousin there, and even if everything he told me were only half true, I figured it should satisfy this pair of picky anthropologists. 'I should have brought you here straightaway.' I said, not entirely meaning to say it aloud. 'It was selfish of me.'

She smiled, and instructed Fen not to kill us before we got there.

After several hours I saw the tributary we needed to take. Fen turned us toward it, letting in a little water on the port side. It was a narrow stream of yellowish brown. The sun disappeared and the air was cool on our faces.

'Water's low,' Fen said.

'You're all right,' I said, scanning for glimpses of the bottom.

The rains hadn't come yet. The banks here rose high, walls of mud and coiling white roots. I watched carefully for the break Teket had told me about. He'd said it was soon after the turn. In a motorized boat it would come fast.

'Here.' I pointed right.

'Here? Where?'

'Right here.' We were nearly past it.

The boat lurched, then slid into a tiny dark canal between what Teket called kopi, bushes that looked like freshwater mangroves.

'You cannot be serious, Bankson,' Fen said.

'They're fens, aren't they?' Nell said. 'Fen among the fens.'

'This is a fen? Jesus, help us,' he said. The passage was wide enough for only one canoe. Branches scraped our arms and because we'd slowed down, insects came at us in clouds. 'You could get bloody lost in here.'

Teket had told me there was only one path through. 'Just follow the water.'

'Like I'm going to do anything else. Fuck, the bugs are thick.'

We motored through this close corridor a long time, their trust in me weakening by the minute. I wanted to tell them everything I'd heard about the Tam, but best to have them arrive discouraged.

'Sure you have enough petrol for this?' Fen asked.

And just then the passage opened up.

The lake was enormous, at least twelve miles across, the water jet black and ringed by bright green hills. Fen pulled up on the throttle to idle and we swayed there for a moment. Across the water was a long beach, and, mirroring it in the water twenty yards offshore, a bright white sandbar. Or what I thought was a sandbar, until all at once it lifted, broke apart, and thinned into the air.

'Osprey,' I said. 'White osprey.'

'Oh my, Bankson,' Nell said. 'This is glorious.'

7

I didn't meet Helen Benjamin until 1938 when we both attended the International Congress of Anthropological and Ethnological Sciences conference in Copenhagen. I went to her panel discussion on eugenics, at which she was its only opponent and the only one who made sense. The way she spoke and moved her hands reminded me of Nell. I rose as soon as the discussion was over and made for the door. But somehow she got down off the stage and overtook me in the entrance hall before I could slip away. She seemed to know all my feelings, and merely thanked me for coming to her panel and handed me a large envelope. It was the kind of thing I'd grown used to, people hoping I'd help them publish their manuscripts, but from Helen it made no sense. Her *Arc of Culture* had been a great success, and whatever acclaim I had garnered by then, with the Grid and my book on the Kiona, owed a significant debt to her work.

I didn't open the packet until I was on the train back to Calais. Such a cavalier gesture, my hand reaching into that brown envelope. It was not a manuscript. It was a booklet made of white typing paper covered by bark cloth, folded in half and sewn down the middle seam. Attached with a paper clip was a note from Helen: *She made one of these each time she arrived in a new place, and kept them tucked in the fabric liner of a trunk, away from prying eyes. I have kept the others, but I thought*

74

you should have this one. There were no more than forty pages, a good many blank at the end. The writings spanned three and half months, beginning with her first days on Lake Tam.

1/3

1/4 Stitched up this new book yesterday then was too intimidated by all these fresh empty pages to put down any words. I wanted to write about Bankson but felt I shouldn't. Wrote Helen instead & managed not to mention him once. My body feels better. Pitiful that a great amount of my pain disappeared when someone paid a bit of attention to it.

This temporary house they've given us is called the House of Zambun. Or maybe I should spell it Xambun—more Greek sounding. From the way they say it, Xambun, low & hopeful, as if its utterance could bring something powerful closer, I am certain it's a spirit or ancestor, though I can't feel anything in here the way I have in other houses reserved for the dead. And if it is a spirit, why would they let us desecrate its house?

I want to write more but too many feelings are bottlenecking somewhere near my collarbone.

1/6 But what was all the fuss about him anyway? If he was ever cold or arrogant or territorial his 25 months with the Kiona must have knocked it out of him. Hard to believe the stories about the string of broken hearts he's left back in England. Plus Fen says he's a deviant. What I saw was a teetering, disheveled, unaccountably vulnerable bargepole of a man. A skyscraper beside me. I'm not sure I've seen such height & sensitivity paired before. Very tall men are so often naturally removed and distant (William, Paul G., etc.). I am wearing his dead brother's glasses.

We were standing in the shallows yesterday waving him off and I remembered a fall day when I was about 8 or 9 and my brother & I had played with some new children in our neighborhood for the first time and we were being called to dinner and we stood in the yard with them chilled by the sudden evening but warm from running and I had a terrible fear that we'd never play like that again, that it would never be the same. I don't remember if my premonition proved true. I just remember the stonelike weight in my chest as I went up the back steps.

I am tired tonight. Trying to learn another language—3rd one in 18 months—probing a new set of people who but for the matches & razors would rather be left alone—it has never felt more daunting to me before. What was it B said? Something about how all we're watching is natives toadying to the white man. Glimpses of how it really was before us are rare, if not impossible. He despairs at the deepest level that this work has no meaning. Does it? Have I been deluding myself? Are these wasted years?

1/10 I think I have made a friend. A woman named Malun. She came by today with some lovely little coconut shell drinking cups for us, a few cooking pots, & a full bilum bag of yams & smoked fish. She speaks several local languages but only a small bit of pidgin so we mostly flapped our arms and laughed. She is older, past childbearing, head shaved like all married women here, muscular & stern until she breaks into giggles which seem against her strong will. By the end of the visit she was trying on my shoes.

I went down this afternoon to see how our real house is coming along. I like the spot we chose, right at the intersection of the women's & men's roads (the men of course have the best water views) where we will be able to keep an eye on the action. There are about 30 people on the job at this point and Fen boss-ing every last one of them around with only a handful of Tam words but a big barking voice when he needs it. So glad it is not directed at me.

Slowly winning over a few children. I go up to the field behind the women's sleeping houses where they play or down to the lake where they swim and I squat on the ground and wait. Today I brought a bright red toy train and pushed it through the sand, making it rumble. Their curiosity was stronger than their fear and they approached until I said "Toot toot!" and they scattered and I laughed and eventually the train lured them back. I added at least 50 new words to my little lexicon while I sat with them. All the body parts plus landscape terms. They don't tire as adults do explaining things. They like to be experts.

And these are little kids 3 to 8 maybe. They're an independent bunch, so different from the Kirakira with their protective adolescent guardians. Here those older girls are meant to start fishing & weaving by 9 or 10 it seems, and the boys apprenticing in the pottery & painting trades. So the little children roam free. Oh little Piya & Amini with their round bellies & tulip bark belts. I just want to scoop them up and carry them about, but for now they keep several yards between us, wary, looking up the beach, making sure there is an adult within sight.

1/11 This afternoon Fen brought home a houseboy, a shoot boy & a cookboy. He had his pick down at the construction site, though the shoot boy seems too delicate to bring us much more than a duck or a shrew and the houseboy Wanji tied a dishrag on his head and raced off to show his friends and never came back. But the cookboy saw the yams & the fish and got to work without a word. His name is Bani and he is serious & quiet and I think a bit of a misfit here among the loud chatty men. If he were a little older he'd make a good informant, but I don't think he's more than 14. Fen & I haven't had the informant battle yet. I told him today at lunch that he could have first pick. He said it didn't matter who he picked because he'd just want who I had in the end. So I said he could choose then I'd choose then he could choose again. We had a laugh about it. I told him that my next book would be *How to Handle Your Man in the Bush*.

I have found a language teacher. Karu. He knows some pidgin from a childhood spent near the patrol station in Ambunti. Thanks to him my lexicon has over 1000 words in it now & I quiz myself morning & night though part of me wishes I could have more time without the language. There is such careful mutual observing that goes on without it. My new friend Malun took me today to a women's house where they were weaving & repairing fishing nets and we sat with her pregnant daughter Sali & Sali's paternal aunt & the aunt's four grown daughters. I am learning the chopped rhythm of their talk, the sound of their laughter, the cant of their heads. I can feel the relationships, the likes & dislikes in the room in a way I never could if I could speak. You don't realize how language actually interferes with communication until you don't have it, how it gets in the way like an overdominant sense. You have to pay much more attention to everything else when you can't understand the words. Once comprehension comes, so much else falls away. You then rely on their words, and words aren't always the most reliable thing.

1/13 Have just spent 4 hours typing up 2 days' worth of notes. Completed census today, 17 houses, 228 people. Had to pry Fen away from housebuilding to get the numbers from the men's houses, which I cannot enter.

Every now and then, if I am not careful, I think of B patching me up that first night and everything goes a little wobbly inside me for a few seconds. It is probably good that he has not come back as soon as he promised he would.

1/17 Malun came over today with an enormous basket and a very serious expression on her face. Xambun, she explained, is her son. She opened the basket and showed me hundreds of lengths of knotted palm fronds, a knot for every day he's been gone. I felt like I grew 4 new ears trying to piece together what she was telling me. It took a while, but I learned that Xambun is not dead. He was lured away by blackbirders to work in a mine, Edie Creek is my guess. He is a big man, a tall man, a wise man, a fast runner, a good swimmer, an excellent hunter, she told me. (Both Bani & Wanji have since confirmed these things and more. Xambun seems to be their Paul Bunyan, George Washington, & John Henry all in one.) Malun wanted to know if we knew the men he went off with. I'm starting to think this is why they took us in so readily, they thought we had information about Xambun. I wish we did. What a treasure trove a man like that would be, what perspective he would have on his own people. Malun believes he is coming home very soon. I didn't have words or the heart to tell her what I know of those gold mines. I didn't tell her he might not be free to leave. Oh the love & fear in her eyes as she stroked her basket stuffed with knots.

8

I had three objectives when I sat down to write my mother every week.

1) Provide proof that I was still alive
2) Convince her that my work had value and was moving swiftly in the right direction
3) Imply without directly stating that I would rather be in her house in Grantchester than anywhere else on earth.

The first objective was, of course, the easiest. I accomplished it as soon as I typed 'Dear Mother.' The other two required deceit, and she sniffed out duplicity in me like a hellhound sniffs death.

But now there was a fourth objective: Do not mention Nell Stone. Easy enough, you might think. And yet I found it impossibly difficult. Three letters I had already yanked from the typewriter. I crumpled them and tossed them out the window and little Kanshi and two of his pals were knocking them around with cane sticks. I tossed out a fourth and the boys shouted with pleasure and Kanshi's grandmother called out from her mosquito bag that she was napping and could they please go and drown themselves.

I twisted in another sheet of paper.

Dear Mother,

Today I believe is the first of February.
Three months left. Perhaps this letter and I will
arrive at your door at the same time. The garden
will be in full flourish then, and we will sit
for tea beneath the lilacs and juneberries and
all will be right with my world once more.

I hope this letter finds you in sound health,
and that no winter 'flu has reached your door.
Has it been a mild winter?

I feared I'd asked this very question in my last two letters,
but plugged on.

By the time you receive this, winter will be a
distant memory at any rate, and we will scheme
about how to keep the aphids off the Felicia
roses and the Russian vine from climbing too far
up the south side of the house. Summer problems.

As I've mentioned, my focus these past weeks
has been on Kiona death rituals. Yesterday I
went to a mortuary ceremony in which the skull
of a long-dead man was dug up then covered with
clay and refashioned back into a fleshy face with
nose and mouth and chin. The poor artist was
heckled terribly about his rendition of these
features, but finally a portrait was agreed upon
and the mintshanggu was performed. The head was
set on a stage and the men crawled beneath the
platform and played their flutes for the women,

```
who listened stoically, almost trancelike.
And then the women rose and hung up food for
his ghost and sung the name songs of the man's
maternal clan. When I asked how long he had been
dead no one could tell me. There was crying,
not the loud theatrical sobbing of the men at
funerals but a more natural weeping. Natural.
I find I use this word indiscriminately. What
is natural to an Englishman might not be at all
natural to, say,
```

I paused here. I was like a schoolboy in my need to just type the word.

```
an American, let alone a tribe in New Guinea.
```

Her antennae would twitch. She would detect something.

```
I find I am more and more interested in this
question of subjectivity, of the limited lens of
the anthropologist, than I am in the traditions
and habits of the Kiona. Perhaps all science is
merely self-investigation.
```

Why not just mention them?

```
I have had some visitors, fellow anthropologists
who have been, unbeknownst to me, in the region
for nearly as long as I have, a married couple.
He's from Queensland, a broad strapping fellow
```

```
I met in Sydney that time, and she's American,
quite well known but a sickly, pocket-sized
creature with a face like a female Darwin.
```

There. That couldn't put her in much of a state, could it? Yes, it would. It absolutely would. I clutched the top of the page and pulled hard, ripping it in two. Blast her. I dragged out the other portion then wadded them together and tossed the ball out to the boys who, when they saw it, sent up another cheer. Direct violation of objectives #2 and #4. After a certain number of sentences, my letters to my mother now became letters to Nell. My mind was stuck in conversation with her and the feeling of talking to her rang through me, disturbed me, woke me up as one wakes from sudden illness in the middle of the night.

Before I left them, I'd slipped a copy of her book in my bag. I read it as soon as I got back, without stopping. And then again the next day. It was the least academic ethnography I'd ever read, long on description and sweeping conclusions, short on methodical analysis. Haddon, in a recent letter, had mocked the success of *The Children of Kirakira* in America, and joked that we should all bring a lady novelist along on our field trips. And yet she wrote with an urgency most of us felt but did not have the courage to reveal, because we were too beholden to the traditions of the old sciences. For so long I'd felt that what I'd been trained to do in academic writing was to press my nose to the ground, and here was Nell Stone with her head raised and swiveling in all directions. It was exhilarating and infuriating and I needed to see her again.

Several times I'd set out toward Lake Tam but turned back within an hour, having convinced myself it was too soon, they wouldn't be expecting me, they couldn't afford the disruption of a visitor yet. I would be a lurking nuisance lumbering along after them as they tried to do the work of twelve months in seven. If they were closer, I could stop by, have a pretext. Fen had spoken of wanting me to go on a hunting expedition with him within a fortnight, but he would have sent word already if he'd been serious about it.

I suspected Fen didn't have Nell's discipline, but he had a sharp mind, a gift for languages, and a curious, almost artistic way of seeing things. On the beach he'd noticed the way the Kiona turned their canoes sideways, with the fishing gear together in front. They look like pews before an altar in a country church, he'd said, and now I could not see the arrangement any other way.

I felt I loved them, loved them both, in the manner of a child. I yearned for them, far more than they could ever yearn for me. They had each other. They could not know what twenty-five months alone in this hut was like. Nell had been in the Solomons for a year and a half, but she'd lived with the governor and his wife, and had all their friends and visitors for company. Fen had been alone with the Dobu, but hadn't he mentioned going to Cairns for his brother's wedding in the middle of it? Home for him had been within a thousand-mile reach.

Outside the boys had switched to bows and arrows, practicing their shooting on a fast-rolling paw paw. One of the boys' strings snapped and he ran into the bush, pulled up a bamboo stem, and, using only his hands and teeth, stripped out a thin fibre, tied it to his bow, and ran back to the game.

Nell and Fen had chased away my thoughts of suicide. But what had they left me with? Fierce desires, a great tide of feeling of which I could make little sense, an ache that seemed to have no name but want. I want. Intransitive. No object. It was the opposite of wanting to die. But it was scarcely more bearable.

9

1/20 Watching the women out fishing, barely any light in the sky yet. Their boats gliding on the flat black water, silver blue columns of smoke from fires in pots at the stern rise thick and taper to nothing. Some of the women are still wading around up to their chests in the cool water, checking their traps. Others are back in their canoes warming themselves at their small fires.

We got our slit gong beats yesterday. They surprised us with a little ceremony. Fen's is 3 long wallops followed by 2 quick ones. Mine is 6 beats very fast like footsteps, they said, imitating my swift walk. Men from Malun & Sali's clan performed the dances, an old woman beside me complaining that the younger generation hadn't learned the steps properly.

1/24 Our house isn't done yet but the children come to me now in the morning, along with anyone else who wants to draw or roll marbles while suffering my halting interrogations. They laugh at me and imitate me but they do answer my questions. Thankfully Tam words are short—2 & 3 syllables, nothing like the 6-syll. Mumb. words—but I didn't bank on 16 (and counting) genders. Fen writes none of it down, absorbs words like sunlight, and somehow innately understands the syntax. He is making himself perfectly well understood and people are much less apt to laugh at him as he is a man and taller than all of them and the dispenser of most of the salt & matches & cigarettes.

1/30 Our stores have arrived from Port Moresby as well as our mail. One solitary letter from Helen. She probably had 30 from me in the same amount of time. Two pages. Barely worth the postage. Mostly about her book, which is nearly done. At the end she slips in: 'I have been spending time with a girl named Karen, in case Louise has already told you.' Which of course Louise had. A very cool letter. And mine to her still so full of apology & regret & confusion. Sometimes I wake up in the night with the thought: She's left Stanley for me. My heart starts racing—and then I remember that it has all already played out and I see her standing at the quai in Marseille in her blue hat and I see me coming off the ship with Fen. That night at Gertie's when she asked me if I preferred to be the one who loved slightly more or loved slightly less. More, I said. Not this time, she said in my ear. I am the one who will always love more. I didn't say, But I love without needing to own. Because I didn't know the difference then.

There were 3 long pinnaces with our stuff and they must have scraped up their sides getting through those channels. The Tam thought it was a raid and we had a tremendous time calming them down. The sight of so many modern items has changed the way they see us (though no signs of Vailala Madness yet) and a good part of me wishes we had just sent for extra paper & the goodies we promised them. But I am grateful for the mattress & my desk, all my work tools, my paints & baby dolls & boxes of crayons so no one has to fight over the purple again, & the modeling clay & cards.

It's been 5 weeks today since Bankson brought us here. He has not come back. He was so good to us that I can't feel resentful exactly. Fen is more openly miffed, claiming B said he'd come back in a fortnight to go on an expedition with him, so Fen could show him the Mumbanyo. We were probably too much for him with our bickering & our whining & all of my maladies. But we are better now. He saw us at our lowest and in some way I think his presence, his enthusiasms about each of us has helped us remember what we like about each other. This leg of the trip has been smoother than the others. I think we will come out of it all unscathed, maybe even with a child. My period is now four days late.

2/1 I understood my first joke today. I was observing the weaving of mosquito bags in the 2nd women's house. I sat next to a woman called Tadi and I asked her what she would do with the shells she earned and she said her husband would use them to buy another wife. 'I cannot make this bag fast enough,' she said. We all fell over laughing.

My mind has circled back again to that conversation with Helen on the steps of Schermerhorn about how each culture has a flavor. What she said that night comes back to me at least once a day. Have I ever said anything to anyone that has come back once a day for 8 years? She had just returned from the Zunis and I had never been anywhere and she was trying to tell me that nothing we're taught will help us to identify or qualify that unique flavor that we need most to absorb and capture on the page. She seemed so old to me then—36 she would have been—and I thought it would take me twenty years to learn what she meant but I knew it as soon as I got to the Solomons. And now I am engulfed in this new flavor, so different from the light but humorless flavor of the Anapa and the thick bitter taste of the Mumbanyo, this rich deep resonant complex flavor that I am only getting my first sips of and yet how do I explain these differences to an average American who will take one look at the photographs and see black men & women with bones through their noses and lump them in a pile marked Savages? Why are you thinking about the common man? Bankson asked me the second night. What does he have to do with the nexus of thought & change? He turns his nose up at democracy. When I tried to explain that my grandmother was my imagined audience for Children of the KK, I think he was embarrassed for me. These conversations with B keep coming back. Perhaps because Fen doesn't enjoy talking about work with me anymore. I feel him withholding, as if he thinks I'll use his ideas in my next book if he says them out loud. It's wretched now to think of our months on that ship home—the freedom of our talk, our lack of self-consciousness and restraint. It all goes back to this idea of ownership again. Once I published that book and my words became a commodity, something broke between us.

So I play what B & I said to each other in my head like phonograph records. He has been stuck in that brittle English structuralism & head measuring & ant colony analogies, with so little decent field training about how to extract what you need. I fear he has been talking to the Kiona about the weather all these months. He seems to know a great deal about the rains. Which have been mild so far, little more than splatters. I don't like it when they hold back like this. It sets things on edge. Oma muni. It bodes ill. Malun taught me this today. But she was talking about a particularly crooked yam.

2/4 I have gone through all the mail now. Lush delightful letters from Mary G & Charlotte. Perfunctory ones from Edward, Claudia, & Peter. Boas made me laugh, saying that missionaries are now rushing in droves to the Solomons to convert their wicked souls. I feel in a daze. Lindbergh baby investigation & the maid swallowing silver polish, Hoover evicting the Bonus Army, Gandhi hunger striking again. And then the book stuff. If I were married to a banker would I be able to relish this success more? Would I be able to show him the letter from the director of the American Anthropological Association or the invitation from Berkeley? All the downplaying I must do starts to rub off on me so that I don't even allow myself a few minutes of private pleasure before the squelching kicks in. But then he surprises me, plucks out the letter from Sir James Frazer and says 'Good onya, Nelliecakes. We've got to frame that one.'

53 letters from readers. Fen read some in funny voices. 'Dear Mrs. Stone, I find it rich irony indeed that you purport to "liberate" our children with your graphic descriptions of behavior, the very reading of which will imprison them in eternal hellfire.' Fen's expression on the word hellfire had me in tears of laughter—it was Mrs. Merne from the ship who tutted about our behavior all the way across the Indian Ocean until she finally got off in Aden. We do well when things are brought round to the ship. Is it always that way with men, that first burst of love or sex the thing that binds you? Do you always have to harken back to those first weeks when just the way he walked across a room made you want to take off all your clothes? So different with Helen. Desire came from somewhere else, at least for me. Someplace deeper? I don't know. I do know I can lie awake all night and it feels as if someone is cutting out my stomach the pain of having lost her is so awful. And I am angry that I was made to choose, that both Fen & Helen needed me to choose, to be their one & only when I didn't want a one & only. I loved that Amy Lowell poem when I first read it, how her lover was like red wine at the beginning and then became bread. But that has not happened to

me. My loves remain wine to me, yet I become too quickly bread to them. It was unfair, the way I had to decide one way or another in Marseille. Perhaps I made the conventional choice, the easy way for my work, my reputation, and of course for a child. A child that does not come. False alarm this month.

2/8 In our own house now. With all our stuff & routine & the smell of fresh wood. I am like an old Victorian lady, receiving my visitors in the morning & going out to the women's houses in the afternoon to do my own calling. My mind slips too easily and often from the children I am meant to study to the women here who are such a contrast to the listless Anapa & coarse but powerless Mumb. women. These Tam women have ambition and make their own money. Yes they give some to their husbands for new wives, or to their sons to pay a bride price but they keep the rest. They do the trading, even of the men's ceramics. And they make their own marital choices, the young men prancing around them like sorority girls. Everything hinges on the decisions the women make. I see fascinating reversals of sex roles here. Fen (surprise, surprise) disagrees.

But he is working more now that the house is done. I have given him a lot of the good stuff: kinship, social structure, politics, technology, religion. He is focusing too much on kinship though, just as he focused too much on religion & totems with the Mumb. He thinks he has cottoned onto some pattern which he refuses to share with me. It does give him direction & energy so I can't complain overmuch.

2/9 Fen & I have just had the fight I've been trying to avoid. Nothing that escalated—he is much better now. It really was a Mumbanyo thing. He has focused on that damn kinship theory to the exclusion of all else so that we now have <u>nothing</u> on government, religion, technology, etc. He suspected it was a cross-sexual rope system, men inherit from their mothers and women from their fathers, and got more & more excited about it, interviewing in the men's houses all day and staying up sometimes all night trying to put it all together. And now it has all crumbled to bits and he refuses to do anything more, won't figure out what the pattern really is and won't work on anything else either. I have asked to trade food & nutrition (which I have already covered sufficiently) for kinship & politics, but he refuses. So I will have to take it all on in secret.

2/10 Thick dreams about Helen in Marseille. Over three years ago now but am still stuck there, going back & forth between the two hotels, trying to split myself in half. H in her blue hat on the quai, her lips quivering: I've left Stanley, her first words to me, and then Fen not giving us the time he'd promised me, coming right up behind me, leaving no doubt, no room for an explanation. Oh rotten days. Rotten. And yet I return to them like an opium addict.

I want too much. I always have.

And all the while I am aware of a larger despair, as if Helen & I are vessels for the despair of all women and many men too. Who are we and where are we going? Why are we, with all our "progress," so limited in understanding & sympathy & the ability to give each other real freedom? Why with our emphasis on the individual are we still so blinded by the urge to conform? Charlotte wrote that rumors are flying about Howard and Paul, and Howard might lose his job at Yale. And her nephew, getting his PhD at Wisconsin, was declared insane and committed to a state asylum when they discovered he was a leader in the Communist Party there. I think above all else it is freedom I search for in my work, in these far-flung places, to find a group of people who give each other the room to <u>be</u> in whatever way they need to be. And maybe I will never find it all in one culture but maybe I can find parts of it in several cultures, maybe I can piece it together like a mosaic and unveil it to the world. But the world is deaf. The world—and really I mean the West—has no interest in change or self-improvement and my role it seems to me on a dark day like today is merely to document these oddball cultures in the nick of time, just before Western mining and agriculture annihilates them. And then I fear that this awareness of their impending doom alters my observations, laces all of it with a morose nostalgia.

This mood is glacial, gathers up all the debris as it rolls through: my marriage, my work, the fate of the world, Helen, the ache for a child, even Bankson, a man I knew for 4 days and may easily never see again. All these pulls on me that cancel one another out like an algebraic equation I can't solve.

2/12 Great commotion on the water this morning. The women's boats which had gone out peacefully earlier came rushing back in shouting & splashing and when I got to the beach I saw that all the screaming had been coming from one woman, Sali, her moans deep and her yelps shrill and then a harsh cry like a mountain lion with an arrow through its flank. She staggered from the canoe to land and crouched in the sand to have her baby. A few of the older women spread bark cloth beneath her. They all began singing songs to lure the baby out. I waited for the taboos to set in and people to be sent away, but no one chased me or anyone else away, not even the few men who had gathered beneath trees behind us. I spotted Wanji among them and sent him up to the house for boiling water & towels. I squeezed in beside Malun.

I assisted in this birth. I saw the baby's head show and retreat, show and retreat like a moon phasing quickly and then suddenly it pushed through the bright red labia all at once while Sali hollered then was so quiet I thought she was dead but then she was screaming again and a shoulder came through, a tiny knob compared to the huge head and at the next ripple of pain I tugged on that little shoulder and the other shoulder came, followed by the belly and the little fat legs and there he was, a baby boy, as if brought in on a tide. Malun & her sister laughed at my tears but I was overwhelmed by life arriving and remembering my sister Katie's fat legs and full of a wild selfish hope that my body having now seen the simplicity of it could manage that someday. Malun bit off the cord and cinched the stump with a reed. Many hands reached out to wipe the white coating off the baby and I wondered if this is where the Mumbanyo's King of Australia myth comes from, the one in which the first man steps out of his white skin. Wanji finally came with the boiled water and towels but we didn't need them. As we walked up the beach Kolun, Sali's husband, came forward and took his child without hesitation and the baby curled up like a kitten in the crook of his collarbone. A few men had flutes and played a formless tune. Sali walked without help and chatted with her two sisters and cousin. I wished I could understand all that she was saying but it was too fast, too intimate.

2/16 Sali's baby died. He wouldn't suck.

2/17 Fen is being insufferable. He cuffed Wanji for taking a few elastic bands without asking and now Wanji is wailing and Fen is shouting and Sali's boy is still dead.

10

She dreamed of dead babies, she wrote in her bark cloth book. Babies on fire. Babies caught in webs of trees. Babies covered in ants. She lay in her bed and counted the number of dead babies she had seen in the past two years. The Anapa boy was the first, cut out of his dead mother's womb so that he would not haunt them. The girl Minalana, nearly a year old, bitten by a redback spider. With the Mumbanyo there was often no death ceremony for infants. You stumbled on them half buried or caught among reeds in the river. Any baby that was an inconvenience or thought to be another man's. And a man could avoid the six-month postpartum taboo against intercourse by disposing of the child. There had been five with the Anapa, seventeen with the Mumbanyo, and now Sali's. Twenty-three dead babies. Twenty-four if she counted her own, a dark clump wrapped in a banana leaf and buried under a tree she'd never see again.

She heard them below the house, waiting for her. Sema's hiccoughy nine-year-old giggle and her little brother's whine, probably for more of the sugarcane that his mother was dangling over his head. She heard the words for eat and sweet and their name for her, Nell-Nell.

She was surprised they still came. They had not attributed the death of Sali's baby to her presence at the birth. Not yet, anyway. When she had visited Sali the night before, she had rested her head on Nell's shoulder for a long time. Her child had been buried two days earlier in a clearing a half hour's walk away. Sali carried him, his tiny body painted with red clay, his face with white, his little chest decorated with shells. In one hand they'd put a piece of sago cake, in the other a child's miniature flute. His father dug a shallow grave. Just before Sali lowered him in, she squeezed a few drops of milk from her full hard breast onto the painted lips and Nell ached for those lips to move but they did not and then they covered him with brown sandy soil.

Fen came in through the mosquito net with a cup of coffee for her. He sat on the bed and she raised herself to take the cup from him.

'Thank you.'

He sat sideways to her, crushed a pale blue weevil with his shoe, stared at the cloth that covered the window. He had a small head, considering his length and girth. It made his eyes and shoulders look bigger than they actually were. His beard grew fast and dark. He had shaved the night before but already it had sprouted back up, not the midnight blue that appeared after a few hours like a storm cloud but real hairs that grew two or three to a pore. Women everywhere thought him good-looking. She had thought him beautiful at first, on that boat on the Indian Ocean.

He knew she'd been crying and wouldn't look at her.

'I just want to keep one child alive.'

'I know,' he said, but did not touch her.

Below they had begun to whap sticks at the supports.

'Where are you off to today?' she said.

'I'm going to help with the canoe.'

Working on the canoe, which he had been doing for the past five days, meant digging out the insides of an enormous breadfruit tree so that eight men could travel inside it. It meant another day without note taking, another day of failing to gather hard information.

'Luro is going to Parambai today, to help settle the dispute about Mwroni's bride price.'

'Who?'

'Mwroni. Sali's cousin.'

'I'm going to help with the canoe, Nell.'

'We just don't have any idea about how they negotiate—'

'It's not my fault you aren't pregnant.'

The lie of it hung between them.

'I keep doing my part,' he said.

I would be seven months along now, she thought. He knew it too.

Behind the scrim she heard Bani fixing Fen's breakfast and singing. She couldn't understand the words. Songs always came last. Often they were strings of names, a line of ancestors, with no breaks between words. *Madatulopanara-ratelambanokanitwogo-mrainountwuatniwran*, he sang, high alto and with tenderness. He could be so serious it was hard to remember he was just a boy.

Bani had told her that he was not a Tam by birth. He was a Yesan, stolen by the Tam in a raid in retaliation for the kidnapping of a Tam girl a Yesan man was in love with. He thought he was less than two when it happened. She asked who raised him and he said many people. She asked who was his family here and he said she and Fen.

'Do you see your mother?' she asked.

'Sometimes. If I go with the women to the market. She is very skinny.'

Nell hadn't understood tinu, skinny, until he sucked in his stomach and pressed his arms to his sides. He had initiation scars from shoulder to wrist and down his back, raised bumps they created by deliberately infecting the cuts.

'What do you feel when you see her?' she asked.

'I feel I am happy I am not skinny and ugly like she.'

'And she? What does she feel?'

'She feels our Tam women ask too much for fish. That is what she says every time.'

Fen's gong signal rang out.

'Bloody hell,' he said, scooting off the mat. 'Why is he so damn slow?'

'Don't be hard on him.'

She heard him tell Bani to put his food in a basket. 'Hurry.'

The noise below swelled as he went down the ladder. She heard their greetings and Fen's *Baya ban* many times. Good day, good day. The children would be reaching to touch his arms and put their fingers in his pockets. His gong beat sounded again and she heard him call in a gorgeous accent she would never possess, *Fen di lam*. Fen is coming.

She got up and put on the shift she'd worn all week, a once white sundress she'd bought on 8th Street for a nickel.

'Meni ma,' she called as she rolled up the window shades.

'Damo di lam,' several called back. We are coming.

'Meni ma,' she said again, for it rarely sufficed to say things just once. The Tam used an operatic repetition when they spoke.

'Damo di lam.'

The house began to shake as people headed up the ladder.

'Damo di lam.'

Luquo came in first. 'Baya ban,' he muttered and only once as he hurried to reach the crayons and the paper and drop into his corner with them. His uncle would come get him within the hour, and scold him for coming here when he was expected to help mix pigments down on the men's road. But Luquo was bored by the years of apprenticing that a boy must put in. He liked to come to the white woman's house. He didn't squat like the others but got on all fours with the paper beneath him, his muscles taut and his naked body swaying slightly as he pressed the crayons hard into the paper. He liked his colors deep and lush and he ground down a crayon as van Gogh was said to flay a brush. She wished she could show him a van Gogh, the self-portraits, for Luquo always drew a portrait, a fierce man in feathers and bones and paint, not a mask, not a head, but the full body of a man. My brother, he said whenever she asked. Xambun, he hollered.

Others liked to talk. Amini, a girl of seven or eight, tried to come up with as many questions for Nell as Nell had for her. Amini wanted to know why she wore all that cloth, why she used a fork to eat, why she wore shoes. And she wanted to know how Nell made all these things she had. Today, as Nell was handing her her favorite doll, Amini asked something she could not understand. Amini repeated it then pointed to Nell's fingers. She wanted to know why she had them all. Few adult Tam had all their fingers. Cutting off fingers was a ritual of mourning a close relative.

'We do not cut our fingers,' Nell said, using the other pronoun for we—nai—she had learned, which did not include the person being spoken to.

Despite this grammatical flourish, Amini smiled the way they all did when she spoke. 'Who do you mourn?' she asked brightly, as if asking Nell her favorite color.

'My sister,' she told her. 'Katie.'

'Katie,' Amina said.

'Katie,' Nell said.

'Katie.'

'Katie,' said a few others, some squatting, chewing, drawing, weaving. The old man Sanjo had found one of Fen's cigarettes and chewed on it slowly. Katie, the room murmured. It was like breathing life into something long inert. No one had ever said her name in their house afterward.

There were no women visitors today. There were not often many, as they fished in the morning, but today there were none. And the men who'd come were agitated, scowling, full of complaints.

Old Sanjo pointed to her typewriter in the big mosquito room. His skin stretched across his armpits like a bat's, so thin it was nearly transparent.

She had promised him she would show him how it worked.

'Obe,' she said to him. Yes.

Nearly everyone got up.

'Only Sanjo,' she said.

She took him into the room. He poked at the netting, firm in its wooden frame. He drew back to poke harder.

No, she told him.

He looked all around, tracing the lines of this ten-by-ten frame of netting they were in. He looked like he wanted to leave. Everyone else was peering in, noses against the screen.

She ripped a piece of paper from her notebook and spun it around the platen.

Sanjo, she typed quickly. He stepped back at the noise. Several children screamed. She pulled out the paper and handed it to him. 'You. Sanjo. In English. In my talk.'

He touched the letters she'd typed. 'I have seen this before,' he said. He pointed to her books. 'I did not know it could be my name.'

'It can be anything.'

'They are powerful?'

'Sometimes.'

'I do not want them.'

She realized he saw the letters as part of his 'dirt,' a piece of him like hair or skin or shit that enemies could steal and put a hex on.

'It is not your dirt.'

He handed it back to her.

'I will keep it here,' she said. 'Then it will be safe.'

Fen did not return for lunch, so she was able to get out early on her rounds to the women's houses. She had been visiting these twelve houses for six weeks now. They each contained several families, minus the men and the initiated boys, who slept in the ceremonial houses closer to the lake. Despite her daily progress with the language, she felt she'd reached an unexpected plateau with the women. The men, though harder to access because she was not allowed into their houses, were free with their words, included her in their talk of who would marry whom, and what would have to be paid, and to whom, while the women had far less patience for chatter. She had never known a tribe where the women were more reticent than the men.

Because the rains were late, the road was a desiccated crust, hard as marble underfoot. Ripe fruit exploded when it hit the ground. Hot air blew down from the high trees, their dry fronds cracking against each other. Bugs aimed for her eyes and mouth, looking for moisture.

At the turn in the road she found Fen with a few men, scraping out the last bits of wood pulp from the hollowed trunk with flat rocks. As usual, even for manual labour, the Tam men wore many strings of round yellow shells around their neck, armbands of bamboo fiber, and cuscus fur pubic covering. Their hair was curled and festooned with parrot feathers. The shell necklaces clacked rhythmically as they worked. Three skulls, leather-brown with age, were propped up against a tree nearby to oversee and bless the work of the descendants of their clan. One skull was missing its jaw. Nell looked for it and sure enough, it hung around the neck of Toabun, the clan elder.

'Good day, Fenwick.'

'Good day to you, mum,' he said, straightening up.

The other men stopped their work to watch them.

He peeked into her basket. He'd taken off his shirt, and his chest was shiny with sweat and stippled with bugs and flecks of wood pulp. 'Ah, the usual bribes, er, enticements, I see.'

'They like a sweet canned peach at this hour.'

He was an athletic man, so unlike the men in her family. He'd been a rugby player at school. His father told her, the one time they'd met, that Fen could have played for the Wallabies if he'd wanted to.

'Don't we all,' he said, leaning in and peering down her dress. 'A nice round white peach.' He reached in, but she blocked him. The men behind him wheezed with laughter.

He had begun to do this lately, perform for them in this way.

'What's going on today?'

'What do you mean?'

'Something's going on. Have they said anything?'

He didn't know and didn't care. He kissed her and the men slapped the canoe and cackled.

'Get some work done, Mr. Show-off.'

She took the turn up the women's road and when she turned back, he was bent over the canoe again. There was no notebook nearby. He hadn't even brought it.

Fen didn't want to study the natives; he wanted to *be* a native. His attraction to anthropology was not to puzzle out the story of humanity. It was not ontological. It was to live without shoes and eat from his hands and fart in public. He had a quick mind, a photographic memory, and a gift for both poetry and theory—he had wooed her with these qualities night and day for six weeks on the boat from Singapore to Marseille—but they didn't seem to give him much pleasure.

His interest lay in experiencing, in doing. Thinking was derivative. Dull. The opposite of living. Whereas she suffered through the humidity and the sago and the lack of plumbing only for the thinking. As a little girl in bed at night, when other girls were wishing for ponies or roller skates, she wished for a band of gypsies to climb up into her window and take her away with them to teach her their language and their customs. She imagined how, after a few months, they would return her home and after the hugs and tears she would tell her family all about these people. Her stories would go on for days. The pleasurable part of the fantasy was always in the coming home and relating what she had seen. Always in her mind there had been the belief that somewhere on earth there was a better way to live, and that she would find it.

In *The Children of Kirakira* she described for a Western audience the way one tribe in the Solomon island of Makira raised their children. In the final chapter, she made a few brief comparisons between Kirakira and American child-rearing customs. She submitted her manuscript not to a university press but to William Morrow, where it was quickly accepted. Mr. Morrow suggested she expand those comparisons into a couple of chapters at the end, which she did, and happily, for it was what interested her most, but it became the sort of opining that hadn't been done in ethnographical writing before. Americans, she discovered upon publication, had never considered the possibility of another way to raise children. They were astounded by Kirakira children paddling in boats alone at age three, still sucking on their mothers' breasts at age five, and, yes, disappearing into the forest or down onto the beach with a lover of either sex at age thirteen. Her research had been a bit too graphic for a general readership, and her theory that adolescence didn't have to be full of the misery and rebelliousness it was in America got lost in the uproar. Fen liked the money the book brought in, but he had planned on *his* name becoming a household word, not hers. But he hadn't written anything more than a short monograph about his Dobu.

In her grant proposal, she claimed that she would continue her inquiry of child-rearing in primitive cultures, but the Tam were tempting her with something even more enticing. At first she dared not hope, but the data kept coming: taboo reversals, sisters-in-law on friendly terms, emphasis on female sexual satisfaction. Yesterday Chanta explained to her that he could not go to visit his sick nephew in the far hamlet because his wife's vulva would go wandering if he did. They were grand on the word *vulva*. When Nell asked if an elderly widow would ever marry again, several people said at the same time: 'Has she not a vulva?' Girls themselves decided whom they would marry, and when. Fen disagreed with every conclusion she drew on this topic. He said she was blinded by her desire to see them this way, and when she laid out her evidence he said whatever power the women had was temporary, situational. The Tam had been chased out by the Kiona and only recently restored to their lake by the Australian government. Many of their men had been killed or calaboosed or blackbirded, he said. Whatever she saw was a temporary aberration.

She decided to go to the last house first today. She was often depleted by the time she got there, and her notes on those families were always less substantial than the others.

'Baya ban,' a little girl called from the first house.

'Baya ban, Sema.'

'Baya ban, Nell-Nell.'

'I'm not coming . . .' Nell couldn't finish the sentence. She didn't know the word for *yet*. 'Fumo,' she said finally. Later.

'Baya ban, Nell-Nell.'

No one seemed to be home at the other houses she passed. No smoke rose from their roofs, no one leaned out of the doorway to call a greeting. Some children were playing a game behind the houses. She could hear their bodies snapping through the brush and then a collective scream when someone was caught. At first her presence had stopped their games. The same children who played in her house in the morning rushed to hide beneath the houses, spying, giggling, shrieking even. But now they didn't notice, didn't even come to see what was in her basket for them. Now they knew she would come to each of their houses and they would see the goodies later.

From the last house on the women's road smoke was rising. All five fireplaces were being used, and she could hear heavy footfall, more like running than dancing. She heard murmurs but no words. Instead of calling out from below first, she climbed up the ladder without a word. The running footsteps grew louder and the whole house shook. People seemed to be yelling at each other in a loud whisper.

Nell-Nell di lam, she said before she pushed the bark cloth aside and stepped in.

It was dim, all the blinds drawn, and she could see little. There was a high-pitched clattering at the back half of the long house, shells or stones being moved around and women whispering and their bare feet thudding quickly across the floorboards. Malun greeted her and offered her guava juice as she always did. Her eyes adjusted and she could make out mosquito bags laid out down the length of the house, but only the long ones, none for the children. Women, thirty or so, many more than usual, were strewn on the floor. Some had torn nets or half-finished baskets in their laps, but many were doing nothing, which Nell had seen plenty of times among the men but never among the women. The women here were never idle. Some raised their heads and whispered their greetings to her.

Malun returned with the drink. Her face was bathed in sweat. The house held a humidity far beyond the normal tropical damp. As she handed Malun things from her basket, she watched her carefully. Her pupils were dilated and tears of sweat were running down her stomach. She had an odd, enigmatic expression on her face and seemed to be trying hard to concentrate. Nell looked for signs of betel nut, lime powder, and mustard pods—a potent combination she knew the Mumbanyo used for a strong high—but saw nothing. Or perhaps they had some other drug. They were high on something, she knew that much. Some seemed unable to keep a smile from twisting up the sides of their mouths, like her brother at the dinner table after he'd snuck off with a bottle of her father's gin. Her own sweat prickled her face and thighs. She'd worked through her own illness and injury; she'd worked with people who only told her lies, who chatted and laughed through every question, who ignored her, teased her, imitated her. It was all, all of it, part of the job, but this odd conspiracy of sweaty women seemed to press at a tender spot deep in her. She picked up her basket and left. It was silent as she climbed down, but when she was five steps away the house exploded with laughter.

11

Seven weeks. I waited seven full weeks and then I could not wait anymore. I got in the canoe before sunrise and gunned it, slaloming through black clouds of mosquitoes and the occasional croc drifting like a tree limb. The sky glowed a pale green, the flesh of a cucumber. The sun came up suddenly, too bright. It grew hot fast. I was used to the heat, but that morning, even moving swiftly in my canoe, I was overcome by it. Halfway there my vision began to sparkle and blacken, and I had to pull over briefly.

I knew the Tam were already a success by the greeting I got. The women in their canoes in the middle of the lake called out loud hellos that I heard over my engine, and a few men and children came down to the beach and gave me big floppy Tam waves. A noticeable shift from the chary welcome we'd received six weeks earlier. I cut the engine and several men came and pulled the boat to shore, and without my having to say a word two swaybacked young lads with something that looked like red berries woven in their curled hair led me up a path and down a road, past a spirit house with an enormous carved face over the entryway—a lean and angry fellow with three thick bones through his nose and a wide open mouth with many sharp teeth and a snake's head for a tongue. It was much more skilled than the Kiona's rudimentary depictions, the lines cleaner, the colors—red, black, green, and white—far more vivid and glossy, as if the paint were still wet. We passed several of these ceremonial houses and from the doorways men called down to my guides and they called back. They took me in one direction then, as if I wouldn't notice, turned me around and doubled back down the same road past the same houses, the lake once again in full view. Just when I thought their only plan was to parade me round town all day, they turned a corner and stopped before a large house, freshly built, with a sort of portico in front and blue-and-white cloth curtains hanging in the windows and doorway. I laughed out loud at this English tea shop encircled by pampas grass in the middle of the Territories. A few pigs were digging around the base of the ladder.

From below I heard footsteps creaking the new floor. The cloth at the windows and doors puffed in and out from the movement within.

'Hallo the house!' I'd heard this in an American frontier film once.

I waited for someone to emerge but no one did, so I climbed up and stood on the narrow porch and knocked on one of the posts. The sound was absorbed by the voices inside, quiet, nearly whispery, but insistent, like the drone of a circling aeroplane. I stepped closer and pulled the curtain aside a few inches. I was struck first by the heat, then the smell. There were at least thirty Tam in the front room, on the floor or perched oddly on chairs, in little groups or even alone, everyone with a project in front of them. Many were children and adolescents, but there were men, too, and a few nursing mothers and elderly women. People moved across the room with purpose, as if they were in a bank or a newsroom, yet in a distinctly Tam style, weight back and bare feet making a sort of smooth slide forward. Every few minutes I had to turn my head to the side to take in cooler, less fetidly human outdoor air, like a swimmer turning for breath. The smell of humanity—without soaps, without washing, without doctors to remove the rot of teeth or limbs—is pungent even outdoors at a ceremony, but inside, with the blinds down and the fire lit to keep away the bugs, it's nearly asphyxiating. Slowly I became aware, as I did my peering in and sipping of the air behind me, of all their belongings. I'd thought the two hundred porters to get up to the Anapa had been an exaggeration, but now I understood it had to be true.

They had brought bookshelves and a Dutch cabinet and a little sofa. At least a thousand books lined the shelves and spilled onto the floor in great piles. Oil lamps rested on end tables. Two writing desks in the large mosquito room. Boxes and boxes of paper and carbon. Photography equipment. Dolls, blocks, toy trains and rails, a wooden barn with animals, molding clay, and art supplies. And great coffers of things still unpacked. In the smaller mosquito room I could see a mattress, a real mattress, though it did not seem to have a box spring or frame, and sat on the floor looking swollen and out of place. I didn't understand how it was that the Tam weren't pawing over their things, pressing the typewriter keys and tearing pages out of books, as the few Kiona children I'd ever let in my house had done. Nell and Fen had established an order—and a trust—I'd never even aimed for.

Just when I thought I should stop spying and return to the center of the village to find them, a little boy in the corner shifted on his hip and I saw her. She was sitting cross-legged, a little girl in her lap and another brushing her hair. She held up a card to a woman facing her. The woman, whose son was nursing vehemently on a breast that looked tapped out, said something and they both laughed. Nell made a few notes then lifted another card. The Tam had a way of holding their chin out, as if someone were holding a buttercup beneath it, and Nell was holding her chin out this way, too. After she had gone through a small stack of cards, a man came and took the woman's place. When Nell got up to get something on her desk, I saw she'd picked up their smooth glide as well.

The boy who'd moved was the one who saw me first. He hollered and she looked up.

She quieted down her guests and came to the doorway. 'You're here,' she said, as if she'd expected never to see me again. I'd hoped for something a bit warmer. She was wearing Martin's specs.

'You're working.'

'I'm always working.'

'All your things came. And they've built you a house,' I said stupidly.

She was so small, Tam-sized, and I hung over her like a lamppost. Her hair had been brushed out by the little girl into a wild airy froth. Her wrists were too thin, but she looked rested and the color had come back to her face. I felt overwhelmed by the presence of her, which was even stronger in actuality than in memory. It was usually the reverse with me and women. I was aware now of how hard I'd tried six weeks ago not to find her attractive. I hadn't remembered her lips and how the lower one dipped in the middle, brimming over. She wore a blouse I hadn't seen, light blue with white spots.

It made her grey eyes glow. She felt mine somehow, wearing my brother's glasses. But she was formidable now, with her health and her work. She looked like she did not know quite what to do with me.

'I didn't want to miss the euphoria. I haven't, have I? You said it happened at the second-month mark.'

She seemed to stop herself from smiling. 'No, you haven't.' She looked back to the man to whom she'd been showing the cards. 'We'd given up on you.'

'I—' Every face was turned to us and to our strange way of talking. Teket told me it sounded to him like cracking nuts. 'I didn't want to get underfoot.' She continued to look at me through Martin's glasses, which made her eyes comically round. 'Remind me how to say hello.'

'Hello and goodbye are the same. Baya ban,' she said. 'As many times as you can stand it.' Then she turned to face the room. She pointed to me and spoke a few brief staccato sentences, fast but with no ear for the rhythm of the language, which surprised me. She went round the room telling me every person's name and I said *baya ban* and the person said *baya ban* and I said *baya ban* and Nell cut that person short with the next person's name. After she had introduced them all, she called to someone back behind the screen in what I assumed was the kitchen area, and two boys came out, a stumpy naked one with a theatrical smile, and a more reluctant tall one in long shorts, clearly Fen's, tied tight at the waist with thick rope, his razor-sharp shinbones below. I exchanged greetings with each of them. Several of the children were giggling at Bani's outfit and he quickly retreated behind the screen, but Nell called him back.

115

'What were you doing just now, with those cards?' I asked.

'Ink blots.'

'Ink blots?'

My ignorance amused her.

She weaved, and I followed, through the tangle of legs and all her equipment to the large mosquito room. The desk closest to us was layered in papers and carbons, notebooks and file folders. There were a few books open near the typewriter, with sentences underlined and notes in the margins, a pencil resting in the crease of one of them. The other desk was empty save for a typewriter still in its case, and no chair to sit in. I would have liked to sit at the messy desk, read the notes and the underlinings, flip through the notebooks and read the typed-up pages in the folders. It was a shock to see someone else doing my work, in the midst of the very same process. As I looked at her desk, it seemed a deeply important endeavor to me, though when I looked at my own it seemed close to meaningless. I thought of how she had gone straight to my workroom in Nengai, how respectful, almost worshipful, how she'd wanted to help me solve the puzzle of the mango leaves.

She'd realized her hair was floating in the humid human air, and she hurried to plait it back behind her, tying it off with a rubber band in one quick gesture. I could now see the tall stalk of her neck. She handed me the top card in a small stack. It was exactly that, a blot of ink, a mirror image of nothing in particular on either side of the center, though it was not homemade and there was no crease down the middle.

'I don't understand.'

'They're Fen's, from when he studied psychology.' She smiled now at my confusion. 'Sit.'

I sat on the floor and she sat beside me and pointed to the big black smudge with its identical sides. 'What does this appear to be?'

I didn't think 'nothing' would earn me high marks so I said, 'Two foxes fighting over an urn?'

Without comment she flipped to the next one.

'Elephants in large boots?'

And the next.

'Aren't you supposed to refrain from smirking at your patient?' I said.

She forced her lips down. 'Not smirking.' She jiggled the card at me.

'Hummingbirds?'

She put the cards down. 'Holy crow. You can take the man out of biology but you sure can't take the biology out of the man.'

'That is your complete diagnosis, Herr Stone?'

'That is my observation. The assessment is a bit more unsettling. Highly and disturbingly abnormal. Elephants in large boots?' She laughed, hard. I laughed too, and a lightness came over me. I felt as if I could float up to the ceiling.

'How could these possibly be useful here?' I said.

'I find that most anything can shed a little light on the psyche of a culture.'

The psyche of a culture. I nodded, but I wondered what she thought that meant. I wished we could sit alone with a cup of tea and discuss it, but her work was through the mosquito net and I didn't want to disrupt her morning any more than I already had. 'May I observe you with them?'

'Bani is preparing us food. You must be hungry. I'll do two more interviews then we can go find Fen. He'll be glad for a proper lunch.'

She sat back down in the same corner spot beside her notebook and called a woman named Tadi over. I settled against a beam a few feet away. The cards were like everything that has spent time in this climate: faded, fraying, damp, and molding. Each card had the same dent at the bottom in the middle where she held it between her thumb and first two fingers, waiting for a response. And it was a long wait. Tadi stared hard at the card with the foxes holding the urn. She had seen neither a fox nor a Greek urn, so she was stumped. She stared with exaggerated concentration. She was a large woman, a mother of many children by the look of her long nipples and stretched stomach skin, which lay in neat folds like a stack of bedsheets in my mother's linen closet. She had only three fingers on her left hand and four on her right. She wore little decoration, just a thin tulip bark ribbon around a wrist with a single cowrie shell strung through it. Like the other women, she had a shaved head. I could see the quiver of her pulse in a vein on her crown. And when she caught me looking at her, she held my gaze for several seconds before I looked away. The only Kiona females who had ever looked me in the eye were the very young and the very old. For the rest it was taboo. Nell lowered the card and Tadi blurted out something, koni or kone. Nell wrote it down and held up another.

After Tadi came Amun, a boy of eight or nine with a wide smile. Amun looked all around to see who was watching and then he said a word that made his friends laugh and the elders scold him. Nell wrote down the word but was not pleased. Even before she lifted the next card he shouted out another naughty word and she quickly called over a woman who was smoking Fen's Dublin pipe to take his place. Amun crossed the room and draped himself in the lap of a girl who shifted but did not stop her mending of a fishing net to receive him. Nell had the woman, just like the rest, sit right beside her, and she showed her the cards like they were looking at a magazine together.

Their boy Bani brought me a cup of tea and a mound of biscuits. I thought it was far too many until nearly every child in the room leapt up and hovered round me making identical moaning sounds. I broke the biscuits in as many pieces as I could and passed them around.

When she was done, Nell stood up and shooed them all out quite unceremoniously, paddling her hands toward the door. On their way out they put everything back in boxes and the boxes back on the shelves, and within minutes the house was put to rights and the floor was shaking from all the feet going down the ladder.

'You have quite a system.'

Though she was looking at me, she hadn't heard. She was still with her work. She was wearing a tulip bark ribbon, too, just above her elbow. I wondered what they made of this woman who bossed them around and wrote down their reactions. It was funny how it all seemed more vulgar watching someone else do it. I felt like my mother, with this sudden distaste for it. And yet she was good at it. Better than I was. Systematic, organized, ambitious. She was a chameleon, with

119

a way of not imitating them but reflecting them. There seemed to be nothing conscious or calculated about it. It was simply the way she worked. I feared I'd never shake my Englishman Among the Savages pose, despite the real respect I had come to feel for the Kiona. But she with only seven weeks under her belt was more of the Tam than I ever would be of any tribe, no matter how long I stayed. No wonder Fen had grown discouraged.

'Let me just put these back,' she said, holding up the cards and her notebook. I followed her, wanting to see her workroom again, not wanting to miss a step of her process.

She put the cards on a shelf and the notebook beside it. 'Sorry. Hold on,' she said, and flipped open the notebook to add a few more thoughts.

Behind her, on the bottom shelf, were over a hundred of these notebooks. Not fresh ones, but battered ones. A record of all of her days since July of 1931, I imagined. For some reason I felt ill again, hot, with a spray of lights dancing at the edge of my vision. I didn't want to vomit onto her notebooks. I stepped back and heard myself ask a question.

'In the mornings,' she said, but I was no longer sure what I had asked. She described her afternoons visiting all the houses on the women's road. She said she also visited two other Tam hamlets nearby. I asked if she went alone.

'There's no danger.'

'I'm sure you heard about Henrietta Schmerler.'

She had.

'She was murdered.' I was trying to be delicate.

'Worse than that, I hear.'

We were outside by then, on the road heading away from

the lake. The nausea had passed but I was still not quite my-self. The sweat that had covered my body a few minutes ago was now ice cold. 'A white woman is confusing to them,' I said.

'Precisely. I don't think they think of me as entirely fe-male. I don't think rape or murder has ever crossed their minds.'

'You can't know that.' Not think of her as female? I wished I could manage that. 'And murder is one of the first natural impulses any creature has to the unknown.'

'Is it? It's certainly not mine.'

She had fashioned a walking stick for her ankle. It struck the ground beside my left toe with particular force.

'You seem as interested in the women here as in the children, maybe more interested.' I was remembering how quickly she had dismissed Amun.

She and her stick stopped abruptly. "Have you noticed anything about them? Has Teket said anything?'

'Nothing. But I did notice that woman Tadi was free to hold my gaze, and that boy—'

'Didn't have the usual self-possession that you see in boys of that age?'

I laughed at the speed with which she finished my sen-tence. She was looking at me fiercely. What was I going to say about the boy? I could hardly remember. The sun seared the road, no shade, no wind. The curve of her breast through her thin shirt. 'I suppose so, yes.'

She tapped her stick rapidly on the hard dry earth. 'You saw this. In less than an hour you saw this.'

It had been two and a half at this point, but I didn't quibble.

Someone shouted out to her from down the road.

'Oh,' she said, racing on. 'You have to meet Yorba. She's one of my favorites.'

Yorba was hurrying, too, pulling a female companion with her. When we all met up, Nell and Yorba spoke loudly, as if they were still separated by the length of the road. Yorba had the unadorned look of Tam women with her shaved head and one armband, but her friend wore shell and feather jewelry and a hairband of inlaid bright-green beetles. Yorba introduced her to Nell, and Nell introduced me to Yorba, and then the friend, whose name was Iri, and I were introduced, all of which required saying *baya ban* about eighty-seven times. The friend did not look up at me. Nell explained that this was Yorba's daughter, who had married a Motu man and was visiting for a few days. We were still in the full sun and I assumed we would move on to find Fen, but Nell drilled them with questions. The daughter, who could not have been a real daughter as she looked several years older than Yorba, did not conceal her delight in Nell's abuse of the language, her long pauses as she searched for words, then the cascade of them in her toneless accent. Nell was most interested in Iri's perspective on the Tam now that she had lived outside the culture for many years. But both women were carrying large ceramic pots in bilum bags on their backs and pleasure soon gave way to impatience. Yorba pulled at Iri's bracelets. Nell ignored their growing discomfort until Yorba raised both hands as if she were about to push Nell straight to the ground and shrieked what seemed like expletives at her. When she was finished, she took Iri's arm and the two women slid away on their bare heels.

Nell pulled a notebook from a large homemade pocket stitched onto her skirt, and without even moving to a shady spot made four pages of her small hieroglyphs. 'I'd like to get over to the Motu sometime,' she said after she put the notebook away, completely unbothered by the way the conversation had ended. 'I never knew Yorba had a daughter.'

'That couldn't possibly have been her child.'

'It's surprising, isn't it? I had the same feeling.'

'They must use the word indiscriminately, like the Kiona. Anyone can be a daughter: a niece, granddaughter, friend.'

'This was her real daughter. I asked.'

'You asked if she were a blood daughter?' Even the words *real* or *blood relation* didn't always have the same meaning for them.

'I asked Yorba if Iri had come out of her vagina.'

'No, you didn't,' I said finally. I had never heard the word *vagina* spoken aloud before, let alone by a woman in my presence.

'I did. The words I make sure to learn on the first day anywhere are mother, father, son, daughter, and vagina. Very useful. There's no other way to be certain.'

She began walking again, and we turned up a small path and she thrashed her stick through the brush, which I felt would anger the snakes more than scare them off. When I walked through the brush I tried to make myself as inconspicuous as possible.

We came to a small clearing, the last piece of flat land before the jungle began. Fen was sitting up against a stump watching some men whitewash a freshly made canoe with seaweed juice. No notebook, knees bent, twisting and untwisting a stalk of elephant grass. The men sensed us first, and said something to Fen, who scrambled to his feet and bounded over.

'Bankson.' He'd grown a thick black beard. He hugged me as he had done in Angoram. 'Finally, man. What happened to you?'

'I'm sorry I've come unannounced.'

'Footman's got the day off anyway. You just get here?'

'He did,' Nell said. 'Bani is making us a nice lunch. We've come to fetch you.'

'That's a first.' He turned back to me. 'Where have you been? You said you'd be back in a week.'

Had I? 'I thought I should give you some time to settle in. I didn't want to—'

'Listen, we're the ones in your territory, Bankson, not the other way round,' he said.

This business of the Sepik being mine infuriated me. 'We need to put an end to this right now, an end to this nonsense.' I was aware that my voice was coming much harsher than I meant, but I couldn't manage to modulate it. 'I have no more right to the Kiona or the Tam or the Sepik River than any other anthropologist or the man on the moon. I do not subscribe to this chopping up of the primitive world and parceling it out to people who may then possess it to the exclusion of all others. A biologist would never claim a species or a wood to himself. If you haven't noticed, I have been desperately lonely here for twenty-seven months. I did not want to stay away from you. But nearly as soon as I left here I felt that my use to you had been exhausted and that you did not need me lurking around. My height can be disturbing to certain tribes.

124

And I am bad luck in the field, utterly ineffective. I couldn't even manage to kill myself properly. I stayed away as long as could, and it is only now I see I have been rude by not coming sooner. Forgive me.'

The spangles returned at that moment from all sides, and my eyeballs ached suddenly and painfully.

The world dimmed, but I was still standing. 'I am perfectly well,' I said. Then, they told me later, I fell to the ground like a kapok tree.

12

2/21 Bankson returned then fainted dead away on the women's road and now he lies burning with fever in our bed. We soak him with water then fan him with palm leaves until our joints ache. He trembles & shudders & sometimes slugs the fan across the room. Can't find the thermometer anywhere but I think it's a very high fever—or maybe it just seems so because of his Englishman's skin. He has a flushed but plucked-goose look to him without his shirt on. His nipples look like a little boy's after a cold swim, two hard tiny beads in his long torso. He sleeps & sleeps and when he opens his eyes I think he's fully conscious but he's not. He speaks in Kiona and sometimes in little phrases of French in quite a good accent. Fen grumbles about how Bankson avoided us all these weeks then shows up sick, how he didn't want to be in our way but is now delirious in our bed. I can see that his complaining is worry. His sharp words, fierce looks—all concern, not anger. Sickness frightens him. It's how he lost his mother after all. I'm seeing now from this vantage point that all the times he's hovered over the bed, scolding me, hounding me to get up, it's been fear, not fury. He doesn't think I'm so weak. He's just terrified I'll die on him. I tell him B's fever will break in a day or two and he lists all the people, whites & natives, we have known or heard about who have died from one of their malarial flare-ups. I've got him out of the house now, sent him off with Bani for water. It's hard to get B to drink. He seems scared of the cup. He bats it away like the fan. I know he's a bit scared of his mother so a few minutes ago I lifted his head and said in my best British battle-axe: "Andrew, this is your mother speaking. You will drink this water," and I wedged the cup between his lips and he drank.

2/23 Fever has not broken. We are trying everything. Malun comes with soups & elixirs. She shows me the plants they are made from but they aren't familiar to me. Bankson would be able to identify them. But I trust Malun. I feel calmer the minute she walks in. She holds my hand and feeds me her steamed lily stems which she knows I love. I have never had a mothering friend in the field before. I am so often the mother, in all my relationships, really. Even with Helen. Today Malun brought the medicine man Gunat who placed charms—little bits of leaves and twigs—in the corners of the house and sang a song through his nose. The Loud Painful Nasal Song, Fen called it. If it doesn't kill you, nothing will. Gunat worried that the mosquito netting is trapping the evil spirits but Fen got him out before he started tearing it down.

I haven't managed to feed B more than 2 spoonfuls of the broth Malun brought. Fen hasn't either. But he has stuck with it. Hasn't run away on an expedition.

He's been right here, insisting that I continue with my rounds in the afternoon, changing B's sheets and placing wet cloths on his forehead and helping him to the chamber pot (a big calabash gourd). All this nurturing has erased doubt and reassures me that he will be a good father—if ever that day comes.

2/24 Fen found a Kiona navigational chart in B's boat. It is such an intriguing thing, a crisscross of thin bamboo slats with small snail shells tied on in certain places. You hold it up to the night sky and align the shells with the stars to locate your position. It is the most exquisite instrument. I've not seen another like it. I wish the three of us could paddle out tonight and get all turned around and use it to find our way back.

2/26 B was quite lucid this morning, apologizing profusely and trying to get out of bed, insisting he should leave us be. But we settled him back down and he's been asleep or delirious ever since.

2/27 Bankson had some sort of seizure while I was out. Fen is shaken & exhausted but won't let me relieve him, won't leave his bedside, keeps talking and talking, a sort of reverse Scheherazade, as if his words will keep B alive.

13

Time stretched like a hair being pulled from each end, every second closer to the snap. Taut. Tauter. Tauterer. Everything was orange. My fingers played in the fringe of a pillow on my grandmother's bed. Orange pillow. England. I was a little boy. A little boy with a little stiffie. It tented the sheet if I didn't press it down. A sluglike insect the size of a toy automobile rolled over me, leaving wet tyre treads. It was hot it was cold it was hot. Huge orange faces bent toward me, flickered away. I couldn't always reach them. Tears leaked from my eyes. My penis ached and ached. I rolled over and it slid into a frozen yam, tight and cold, and I fell asleep, or into another sleep. I dreamt of my bucket behind Dottie's house: wooden, streaked with green mold, wire handle that bit into your skin when it got heavy. I dreamt I had hands with missing fingers. There were people hovering about I knew I should recognize but did not. My eyeballs weighed ten stone each. When I shut my eyes I saw whorls of an ear, a giant ear, and I had to force the lids up again to get away.

There's a worm in my winky, I thought.

'Is that so?' a lady replied. She sounded like she was smiling. I didn't think I'd said it out loud. Even though I was certain my eyes were open to avoid the giant ear, I couldn't see if it was Nanny putting on a funny accent.

John was in France, not Belgium, naked on a country road. Martin came out from behind the shrubbery and covered him up with my father's linen jacket. I called out to them but they did not turn. I screamed and screamed for them. I tried to run but a bearded man pinned me down, took out a knife, and delicately scraped the blowfly larvae from sores on my stomach.

Whatever you do, Andrew, my mother told me once, do not go around boring people with your *dreams*.

I do not know if it was hours or days before I was able to identify where I was. It was nighttime, and I was aware of cigarette smoke and the sound of a typewriter. My room was dim but I could see down the long house and into the other mosquito net where a woman with a braid down her back, a dark braid against a white shirt, was typing. A man stood beside her, smoking. Then he leaned down, his hand with the cigarette at the back of her chair, to see her words. Nell. Fen. I felt such a relief upon recognizing them, like a child identifying Mother, Father.

'Jesus, Bankson, you febrile wanker.' He shoved me one way then the other, tossed someone the mess, and found another set. 'Can you sit up?'

'Yes,' I said, but I couldn't.

'Never mind.' He pushed me around again and there were fresh sheets below and above me. His face shimmered with sweat. There was a chair by the bed and he sat in it. He held a cup of water out to me. I tried to bring my lips to it but I couldn't reach. He nudged a hand under my head and lifted my head toward the cup and held it there as I drank. 'Good. Good,' he said, and lowered me back down.

'Do you want to sleep some more?'

Had I been sleeping? 'No.'

'Hungry?'

'No.'

The cloth window shade was rolled up and through it came voices, mostly children's voices, and a hot wind. A young man was walking down to the water with a twisted white bundle. Wanji.

'Let's talk,' I said. I propped my head up at a sharper angle.

'What do you want to talk about?' He seemed amused by the idea.

'Tell me about your mother,' I said. I was thinking of my mother, the way she was in my youth, and of her kitchen apron and her wide cool hand on my forehead and the powdery orange smell that came up from her underarms.

'No. I don't want to talk about that.'

My head began to hurt and I could not think of another subject. Tell me anything. But before I could say it, sleep pulled me back under. Perhaps I'd left my eyes open, perhaps he didn't care if they'd drooped shut. When I woke up he was talking about the Mumbanyo. 'I saw it again, after they took it back. The day before we left. It was Abapenamo's turn to feed it and he let me follow him.' He had brought the chair even closer to the bed. He was speaking quietly. Two years in the Territories had made us all thin, but Fen's collarbone rose up far too high, curling over the dark hollows at the base of his neck, his face a narrow wedge. His breath turned my stomach and I had to shift away from its stream.

131

'I thought it would just be in some hut a half-mile away but it was at least an hour's hike away, mostly running.' His voice dropped to a scrape. 'I memorized the route. I swear I could get back there. I go through it in my mind every day so I won't forget.' He got up and peered out the window, looking in both directions, then sat back down again. 'There's nothing else like this thing in this whole region. It's hundreds of years old. Big, six feet at least. And it's got symbols, Bankson, logograms carved all the way down the bottom half that tell their stories. But only a few men every generation are taught to read them.'

Even in my head-throbbing stupor, I recognized this as thrilling and impossible. No system of writing had been discovered among any tribe in New Guinea.

'You don't believe me. But I know what I saw. It was daylight. I held it. I touched it. I made drawings afterward.' His chair squeaked and then he was back with pages. He'd used Nell's crayons. 'I swear this is how it looked. See these?' He pointed to a band of what looked like circles, dots, and chevrons. It hurt to move my eyes so much. 'Look at this. Two dots in the circle. Means woman. One dot, man. This V here, with the two dots, crocodile. Abapenamo explained them all to me. Grandfather, war, time. All logograms. This means to run. They have *verbs*, Bankson.' He was a good artist. The flute was fashioned in the shape of a man, with a large angry painted face and a black bird perched on its shoulders whose long beak curled over his head and was boring into his chest. Down below was an erect unsheathed penis. And below that, according to Fen, were vertical rows of writing.

'Have a look here.' He shuffled the pages. 'Here's a map I made that same day. Take us right to it. You took so bloody long to come *back*, we hardly have any time now. We need to go back there and get this thing.'

'Get it?'

There was a creak on the stairs and he jumped up and hid the drawings away where he'd gotten them, in a black trunk on the other side of the bed. The creaking stopped and he looked out the window toward the ladder. A woman was looking for Nell-Nell, and Fen told her where she was, pointing up the road.

'We can't leave here without it. The next time we come, it'll be in a different place. I know where it is now. We could sell it to the museum for a right heap of cash. And then there are books to be written about it. Books that would blow past *Children of the Kirakira*. It would fix us up for *life*, Bankson. We'd be like Carter and Carnarvon discovering Tut. We could do this together. We're the perfect team for it.'

'I don't know anything about the Mumbanyo.'

'You know the Kiona. You know the Sepik.'

My body felt like two hundred more pounds had been laid on top of it and a few poisoned arrows had been shot through my skull.

'I know you're sick, mate. We don't have to talk about it further now. Get better, then we can plan it out.'

I dreamt of the flute, its gaping mouth and sinister bird. I dreamt of nicked ears and Fen's wedgelike face.

Nell fed me from the supply of pills I'd given her. She made me drink. She offered me food but I couldn't take it. The sight of it made my stomach clutch. She did not try to talk to me apart from these basic transactions of liquid and medicine. But she sat in the chair, not close to the bed like Fen but a few feet off my left foot, sometimes standing to place a damp cloth on my forehead, sometimes reading, sometimes using a great fan on me, sometimes looking up somewhere above my head. If I smiled at her she smiled back, and there were times I half pretended, half believed, she was my wife.

I shut my eyes and Nell disappeared, replaced by Fen who sat so much closer, the fan nearly swatting me, the wet cloths runny, water dripping in my ears.

I think he was telling me about his time in London, and it happened just after that. All I can say is that everything that was big got small and everything that was small got big. A great sudden terrifying inverse. I remember not being able to shut my mouth. I remember nothing else after that, just waking up more or less in Fen's arms on the floor. He was hollering things, ropes of saliva coming out of his mouth. A great many people came after that, Nell and Bani and others I didn't know, and I was put back on the bed and when I opened my eyes it was just Fen and Nell and they looked so ghastly worried that I had to shut them again. The next thing I was aware of was Fen shaving my face.

'You were scratching it so much,' he said. 'I thought you'd flaked out on us.' He tilted my head up so he could get underneath my chin.

Through the netting I saw Nell holding him, hushing him, as he shook.

I heard:

'You're so good with him.'

'Better than with you, eh?'

'Methinks you'll be a good papa.'

'Youthinks, but you aren't certain.'

'You had a seizure,' Fen said. 'You stiffened up like a corpse then writhed like a whip snake then stiffened and this yellow shit came out of your mouth and your eyes were gone. Blank white balls like this.' He made an awful face and inhuman noises and Nell told him to stop.

Every bit of me hurt. I felt as if my body had been flung from the top of a New York skyscraper.

My fever broke. That's what they told me. They brought me plates of food and seemed to expect me to leap out of bed.

I woke and my eyes were already open and Fen was talking. We seemed to be in the middle of a conversation. I had become a receptacle for his whirring thoughts, and he didn't particularly mind if I was awake or asleep, lucid or befuddled. 'My brothers were trouble, every one of them. But I was the least favorite child. I was small and smart. I used words in ways that bothered my parents. I liked books. I wanted books. My teachers praised me. My parents walloped me. I hated farm work. I wanted to leave home before I had words for the thought. In some ways I would have been better off if I had just run away then, age three, just packed a little bag and troddled on out to the main road. Not sure things could have been much worse. We were raised to know nothing, to think nothing. Chew our cud like the cows. Say nothing. That's what my mother did. Said nothing. I made myself as useless as possible in order to stay in school. I was the only one who did. I was lucky to have three brothers ahead of me, otherwise my father never would have allowed it.'

'And a sister,' I remembered.

'She was younger. At school I received something somewhat close to affection. At home, even when I managed to beat my brothers at something, I got ridicule. Then my mother died and it got worse.'

'How did she die?'

He paused, unused to my participation. ''Flu. Gone in five days. Couldn't breathe. The sound of it was terrible. The only thing I saw through the door before my aunt pulled me away was a bare foot sticking out the side of the bed. It was pale blue.'

In those hours or days it seemed I fell asleep and awoke to the sound of his voice.

'I was pretty well out of my head when I got on that ship. Twenty-three months with the Dobu sorcerers and then a few days in Sydney where I proposed to a girl I thought had been my girlfriend and she turned me down. A Dobu witch had put a love hex on me before I left them, but so much for that, eh? I didn't want anything to do with women or anthropology at that point. That first night on board I heard Nell holding forth at a big table at dinner and I figured she'd had this brilliant field trip and some stupid revelations about human nature and the universe, and it was the last thing I wanted to listen to. But I was virtually the only young man on the ship and some meddling old biddies arranged for me to dance with her. The first thing she said to me was 'I'm having trouble breathing properly.' I told her I was, too. We were both having some sort of claustrophobia being enclosed in those rooms. As soon as we could break away, we took a walk on deck, the first of many. I think we must have walked a hundred miles on that voyage. She had a fellow meeting her in Marseille. I wanted her to stay on with me to Southampton. She didn't know what to do. She was the last off the boat and the fellow saw me and knew I'd got her. I saw it in his face.'

'She had the body of a tart. Nothing like my mother's. Full breasts, narrow waist, hips made for a man's hands. I had the horrible suspicion that my brothers and I had created that body, that if we had not done what we had done she wouldn't have developed the way she did.' His voice was so low I could barely make the words. 'Christ, that farm was out in the middle of fucking nowhere. No one had any idea what was going on. Except my mother. She knew. I know she knew.' His voice split then and he looked up to the rafters and pinched off his tears. His face looked like that black bird was boring into him. Then he reached down and lit a cigarette and said, quite calmly, 'Nothing in the primitive world shocks me, Bankson. Or I should say, what shocks me in the primitive world is any sense of order and ethics. All the rest—the cannibalism, infanticide, raids, mutilation—it's all comprehensible, nearly reasonable, to me. I've always been able to see the savageness beneath the veneer of society. It's not so very far beneath the surface, no matter where you go. Even for you Pommies, I'll bet.'

I heard them on the mats they'd set up in the large mosquito room beside their desks. The mats creaked and snapped. Whispering. Breathing. The unmistakable rhythm of sex. A cry cut short. Laughing.

Daylight and he was yelling. I turned and saw him towering over Bani, who was crouched by the dining table. Fen smacked him on the ear and he fell over whimpering, curled in a ball.

'Where's Nell?' It felt like days since she'd sat in the chair.

'Out counting babies. She thinks I'm doing such a stellar job she's promoted me to head nurse.'

He was shaving me again.

'You're like a bear,' he said, though he was far furrier than I.

He smelled of cigarettes and whiskey, the smell of Cambridge and youth. I didn't need a shave, didn't particularly want a shave, but I breathed in the smell of his hands and breath. He wiped me with a dry towel.

'You have three freckles, right below your lip.' He was drunk, quite drunk, and I felt lucky I hadn't been cut. He leaned in to touch the freckles and kept leaning until his mouth was on mine. I barely had to press a hand on his chest and he sprung back, wiping his lips as if I had initiated it.

Nell read from *Light in August*, which a friend had sent her a few months ago. Fen lay on the bed beside me and Nell read from the chair with a bit of hauteur, the same sort of pretension American actresses had when they spoke their lines. She was self-conscious, reading aloud, in a way she wasn't at all in regular life, when the words were hers.

Fen and I caught eyes after the first sentence. He pulled a face and she caught me grinning.

'What?' she said.

'Nothing,' I said. 'It's a good book.'

'It is, isn't it?'

'It's naïve tendentious American drivel,' Fen said, 'but go on.'

He was so much at ease with me that I began to wonder if I'd hallucinated the kiss. After Nell stopped reading she climbed on the bed too and we lay there the three of us watching the bugs try to claw their way into the net and talking about the book and about Western stories compared to the stories told here. Nell said she'd gotten so sick in the Solomons of hearing their pigman creation myths and their enormous-penis myths that she told them the whole story of Romeo and Juliet.

'I really dragged it out. I acted out the balcony scene, the stabbings. Of course I set it all in a village much like theirs, with two rival hamlets and a healer instead of a friar, and that sort of thing. It's a tribal tale to begin with, so it wasn't hard to make it familiar to them.' She was on her side and I was on my side facing her and Fen was on his back between us so I could only see half her face. 'So finally—and it took me well over an hour in that stinking language; six syllables a word!—I got to the end. She's dead. And do you know what the Kirakira did? They laughed. They laughed and laughed and thought it was the funniest joke ever told.'

'Maybe it is,' Fen said. 'I'd take a pigman story any day over that rubbish.'

'I think it's the irony they're responding to,' I said.

'Oh, no doubt.'

Ignoring him, Nell said, 'Funny how irony is never tragic to them, only comic.'

'Because death is not tragic to them, not in the way it is to us,' I said.

'They mourn.'

'They feel sorrow, great sorrow. But it isn't tragic.'

'No, it isn't. They know their ancestors have a plan for them. There's no sense that it was wrong. Tragedy is based on this sense that there's been a terrible mistake, isn't it?'

'We're sort of big dramatic babies in comparison,' I said. She laughed.

'Well, this baby's got to take a piddle.' Fen got up and went down the ladder.

'Please use the latrine, Fen,' Nell called.

But he must not have moved more than a foot from the house before his stream hit the ground with great force.

'This will go on for a while,' she said.

It did. We were facing each other on the bed.

140

'And then there's going to be—'

Fen broke wind.

'That.'

'Togate,' Fen said quietly, which was Tam for *excuse me*.

We laughed. My head felt clear. Our hands were a few inches apart on the warm spot where Fen's body had been.

14

3/3 Bankson went back today so we had 2 days with him in decent health. We took him to the other Tam hamlets—or he took us in his boat that zips around to the astonishment of all the fisherwomen wading in the water. In the hamlets we were able to cover a lot of ground. Bankson's Kiona is understood by many. He is trying to adopt our ethnographic ways but they don't come naturally to him. You get the sense he would have a hard time asking for a light in a pub. But he's an excellent theorist. We talk & talk. Topics that are sure to cause tension between Fen & me become productive discussions with B there. Fen is more reasonable around him, and maybe I am too. Bankson agrees with my assessment of where the power is accruing—with the Tam women—and we are able to have useful conversations about it, all 3 of us. B is intuitive about F's possessive nature so that I haven't had to say a word, like last night when we were talking about sex roles in the West and B & I fell perfectly in step and I could sense how much further we could take our thoughts, but B rerouted it back to Fen's Dobu at just the right moment. He navigates it as if I had given him a bamboo & shell chart to hold up to us.

Last night he pushed us out the door for a hike. The moon was nearly full and everything lit up silver

and the stars at the edges of the sky were whirling &
dropping so fast and even the bugs looked like chips of
meteorites falling through the air at us. A few people
were out and followed us down the road but when
we veered up the path into the hills they whispered a
warning to us and turned back. The Kirakira weren't
scared of the night but the Anapa, Mumb., and Tam are
all wary of the spirits in the bush who will steal your
soul if you give them half a chance. Bankson collected
some rotten branches covered with something he called
hiri, a fluorescent fungus that cast a pale light on the
ground as we climbed. F & B got into a little male
one-upmanship and we went higher and higher until
we discovered a small nearly perfectly round lake and
the moon bathing right in the center of it. F and B
plunged in. I felt I should hide my inability to swim
from Bankson—he'd be shocked and want to teach
me on the spot and somehow F would take it both as
a criticism and a threat—so I splashed around in the
shallows and we looked at the stars and talked about
death and named all the dead people we knew and
tried to make a song out of all their names.

Bankson told us what he has learned about the
old Kiona raids, how the killer at the end of a battle
stood in his canoe and held up the head of his enemy
and said, 'I am going to my beautiful dances, to my
beautiful ceremonies. Call his name,' and the van-
quished on the beach called the name of their dead
man then cried out to all the victors as they pulled
away, 'Go. Go to your beautiful dances, to your beautiful

143

ceremonies.' Bankson said he once tried to explain the war and the 18 million dead to Teket, who could not comprehend it, the number alone, let alone that many killed in one conflict. B said they never found the whole of his brother's body in Belgium. He said surely it is more civilized to kill one man every few months, hold up his head for all to behold, say his name, and return home for a feast than to slaughter nameless millions. We were standing very still in the water then and I would have liked to hold him.

It is a bit of a dance we three are in. But there is a better balance when B is here, too. Fen's demanding, rigid, determined nature weighs heavily on one side of the scale and Bankson's and my more pliant & adjustable natures on the other, equaling things out. I can't help but think I can use this inchoate theory in my work, that there is something about finding the balance to one's nature—perhaps a culture that flourishes is a culture that has found a similar balance among its people. I don't know. Too tired to think it through any further. Maybe it's just we're both a little in love with Andrew Bankson.

15

Upon my return to Nengai, Teket greeted me on the beach with a note. I knew by the shape of it, the three sideways folds, that it was from Bett. He handed it to me with great relief, as if he had been standing near the water for the entire week I'd been gone. Responsibility weighed heavily on Teket. It wasn't hard to imagine him at Charterhouse, an earnest prefect, a stellar student. He asked me a great number of questions and, because the Kiona elders pass down their knowledge as secret family heirlooms, he treated the information I shared with great care. When an argument broke out between his clan and another about the nature of night, he'd asked my opinion. I told him what I believed about the earth's diurnal rotation and its orbit around the sun. Afterward he coyly referred to it as 'that matter we both know about,' and whenever the sun or the moon came up in conversation among others, he always shot me a special look.

I took the note, but much to Teket's disappointment I put it in my pocket without reading it. From its swollen edges I could tell the page had been folded and unfolded many times and it amused me to think of him studying Bett's small Scottish scratches.

I asked for news, and he told me that Tagwa-Ndemi's baby was a girl so little she fit in a coconut shell, and that a thief greased in palm oil so no one could get hold of him ran through

Teket's aunt's house in the middle of the night, stealing three necklaces and a Turbo shell. Both Niani's sons were ill, but Niani sat up all night negotiating with their ancestors and now they are better. I headed toward my house, but Teket was not finished. The night after I left, he said, Winjun-Mali tried to enter the mosquito bag of his brother's wife, Koulavwan, but her mother heard him and shouted and Winjun-Mali tried to hide among the pots in the house but the mother caught him. He was brought to a ceremonial house where he argued his case. He claimed that he had seen Koulavwan give a betel leaf to her sister's husband and that he was just making sure she was remaining faithful while his brother was away. He said that Koulavwan's vulva was too wide for his taste. When he said this, all of the women who were listening under the house began shouting and Winjun-Mali picked up his spear and jammed it through the floorboards, nicking his own mother's ear and disrupting the proceedings. Then Winjun-Mali's father got in an argument with Koulavwan's father about her extravagant bride price. Koulavwan's father reminded him that when they were boys Winjun-Mali's father had taken the glory for the killing of a man Koulavwan's father had killed for him. He pointed to the tassels on Winjun-Mali's father's lime stick and asked if any of them were for real murders. Before it turned violent, Teket's father cried out that their blood had made the baby in Koulavwan's belly and they must not fight. So, Teket said, we all exchanged areca nuts and went back to bed.

A few months ago I would have been dismayed to miss all this and would have hurried to write it all down, but now I let it wash over and past me, without even trying to catch a drop. He took in a breath to say more but I pointed my fingers to the ground, a signal mothers gave their children to quiet down, and told him he'd have to save the rest for later, that I was too tired. Teket was unable to hide his disappointment, and lingered to show it to me, then finally turned away.

Teket would have liked to have someone like Nell. In her he would have found a kindred spirit, a tireless fellow prefect. They could have spent hours together, Nell cross-examining him about who came from whose vagina, relishing all the details that Teket had saved up for her return.

Alone in my house I lit the fire, placed a pot of water on top, steeped the tea, sat down, and opened the note from Bett.

> Back on the boat. Rabaul insane. Missed you. Where
> are you? No one can tell me. Should I be worried?
> Come find me, sweet.

Four months ago I would already be back in the canoe, heading straight for her pinnace. I blew across my tea. I'd go, of course. I knew that, but I'd go for a different reason now. And Bett would feel it. I knew how it would play out, nothing spoken, everything clear.

I'd go in the morning. After my tea, I unzipped my bag. Wanji had washed my clothing. The shirts were folded perfectly, as if for a shelf in a shop. On the one hand I was disgusted by Nell and Fen's employment of the natives, the way they came in like a corporation and hired up the locals, skewing the balance of power and wealth and thus their own results. But on the other, I saw how efficient it was, how much time it freed up if you weren't making the meals and washing up and scrubbing clothing, all of which I had been doing for

147

myself for the past two years. The night before the three of us had worked together in their office, typing up our notes, while Wanji fetched water and the shoot boy came in with two pigeons and Bani cooked them up in a lime sauce. The sauce was so spicy it made her cheeks glisten, and I had to clasp my hands together so that I did not reach out and touch her skin.

I zipped up the bag and went back down to the water.

Teket, still on the beach, was not surprised. He knew what a piece of this beige paper set in motion. He knew he could expect me back by sunset tomorrow, more blood in my skin and my limbs loose as a boy's.

Bett was in the wheelhouse, eating something yellow from a tin. She looked blankly in my direction, hearing the motor, and when she finally recognized it as mine, she ducked through the small door and waved from the bow.

I shouldn't have come. If there had been any decent way of wheeling my boat around and heading straight back, I would have done.

There had been a husband at one time. They'd been in engineering school together in London, come here to work on a bridge in Moresby, but by the time the bridge was finished, he'd fled to Adelaide with a girl and Bett signed a contract for a bridge in Angoram and bought this pinnace to get herself there. She'd lived on it ever since. I suspected she was close to forty, though we'd never discussed our age.

I cleated my canoe line to her stern and she gave me a hand up. She wore a clean white shirt and smelled like lilies. A new smell.

'You took your time.'

'I just got back this morning.'

'From where?'

'Lake Tam.'

'Hunting?'

I was a horrible liar but said yes.

'Good hunting up Lake Tam?'

She sensed something, perhaps that I hadn't already taken off all her clothes. I lifted my hand halfheartedly to her blouse.

She watched me unbutton it without moving. I liked that. I didn't want her to reach in and find me underenthusiastic. But as I opened up the shirt and touched her nipples with the tips of my thumbs and felt the weight of her breasts in my palms, my body made the shift to this woman, this body, and I felt my determined erection with relief.

She never, for this initial welcoming, led me down to her bed, but took me right there *en plein air* around the ropes and tools and storage boxes. She was warm and familiar and though I wasn't quite myself, eventually I hollered over her shoulder toward the trees, which shook from animals running from the sound. We laughed at a loud frightened *eeeeeeeooooooooooeeeeeee* and our chests stuck and unstuck loudly.

I believed if I could do that twenty more times I might be able to flush Nell Stone entirely out of my system.

She slid down to the floor and we leaned against the box together. We brushed the bugs out of our crotches like monkeys and I asked about her trip to Rabaul and she told me she'd met Shaw's nephew, who was a district officer down south, and we tried to imagine his uncle setting a play in the

Territories. I said the week's events in Nengai would be more than enough material, and told her about the oiled-up thief and Winjun-Mali and his visit to Koulavwan's mosquito bag.

'Why does no one visit me in the middle of the night?' she said. 'The natives just politely paddle past as if the boat were an unremarkable log.'

'Barnaby has nearly the same boat.'

'His is green.'

'They aren't going to approach what they think belongs to a government official. But if you sat out here like this you'd stir up some interest.'

'You think so?' She rolled her naked body onto mine. There was nothing more to say so I kissed her and opened her legs and we moved hard against each other and against the rough wood of the deck. Then she went inside and came out with cigarettes and bathrobes and we smoked until it was time for dinner.

She cooked a barramundi on the grill at the bow and we ate it with mustard and a bottle of champagne she'd gotten in Cooktown. Across the river there was a sudden thrashing and a great spray of water. I made out in the dusk two crocodiles fighting. I saw their snouts high out of the water, jaws open, and then the one on the left sunk its teeth into the tough skin of the other's neck, and they both went below the water, which closed flat over them after a while.

'What was that? Crocs?'

She was squinting. I knew she had terrible eyesight, but I'd never wondered where her specs were, or once thought to offer her Martin's glasses.

*   *   *

I left before sunrise the next day. The water was dull and un-
reflective, the shores silent. She sent me off with a mug of tea
and a box of caramels. Usually she gave me a bottle of whiskey,
and I felt the sweets were an insult, a downgrade of sorts, but
I sucked them one after the other the whole way back.

16

I stayed away from Lake Tam for several weeks, during which time my work went well. I began inviting people to my house, not in the numbers that Nell did each morning, but in small groups. I had Teket's whole family for a dinner of a wild pig we'd shot and pears from tins which Teket had to persuade them were safe and uncursed. His grandmother took a great liking to the pears and their sweet juice, and they carried home the empty cans as if I'd given them a hundred pounds apiece. I had Kaishu-Mwampa, the old woman who wouldn't speak to me, and her grandniece in to tea. They didn't like it, and I told them it was better with milk and they laughed when I tried to describe what milk was because they had never seen a cow. A few days later, Tiwantu announced there would be a full, traditional Wai for the accomplishments of his son after the next full moon. I was having my own small euphoria.

It might have gone on like this—my work in Nengai, a few short trips to Lake Tam—until July, when I planned to leave. But the day after Tiwantu made his announcement, Teket came back from trading with a note in Nell's hand.

17

They awoke to one long scream, followed by a barrage of others. She had no idea what time it was. The sky was black, no edge of light.

In a crisis Fen became even quicker—and feline. He disappeared in one motion down the ladder. She hurried to catch up. The turmoil came from up the women's road. Fen said something but she couldn't hear him.

When they turned the corner, it was as she'd feared, a shrieking mass of bodies. They stopped twenty feet from the outside edge of the crowd, which was facing inward, toward Malun's house. In the dark she could make out the long back of Sanjo and Yorba's thick arms and the little head of Amun, but only briefly. They were all moving, churning, and shouting so loudly it affected her vision. Many had ripped the necklaces and bracelets and waistbands and armbands and hair wraps from their bodies and thrown them on the ground as they hugged and wept and hollered and pressed toward the center, toward whatever was happening through the thicket of bodies.

Fen took her hand and inched closer. He gripped her tighter and pushed into the crowd. 'We have to—' he said, but she lost the rest. Then she lost his hand. Everyone was pressing inward and she was pushed and shoved and poked along with them. She tried to push back, hold her ground, but it was no use. She wasn't sure she wanted to see whatever was happening. But she was being forced toward it, a great muscle of Tam kneading her forward. She couldn't understand why she recognized so few people, why no one recognized her. People were hysterical, and the breath and sweat of so many frenzied bodies was a sour buried-alive smell. She felt certain there would be a dead body in the centre. She hoped it was not a child. Please dear God no more dead children. She wasn't sure if she was screaming this aloud. She tasted vomit and blood but didn't think it was hers. Ahead firelight flickered. And then she saw them, Malun and a man in green trousers. They were standing but he was curled over her and she held him with great effort, his full cumbersome weight, keening as if over a dead body. But he was not dead. There were long deep scars across his bare back, fresher and far cruder than his initiation scarring, lashings without design, but he was not dead.

Come as soon as you get this, Nell's note to me read. Xambun has returned.

18

On the fourth night of the celebration of Xambun's return, Fen came home naked and slathered with an oil that smelled like rancid cheese, claiming he had danced with Jesus, his great-great-grandmother, and Billy Cadwallader.

Nell was at her typewriter, writing a letter to Helen. 'Who's Billy Cadwallader?' she asked.

'You see? That's how I know it's real. Couldn't have made up a name like that. He was just a boy.' He was looking out the door as if these dance partners just might have followed him home. His hair was full of painted clay beads and ash from the fires was caught in the oil on his skin. He planted his feet wide apart to stay upright, but he still swayed. He was pure muscle and bone, like a native. He would never refuse a hallucinogen; he would drink, eat, snort, or smoke whatever was offered to him. 'You know, I think'—he jerked around, beads rattling, smiling at her as if he were just then noticing she was in the room—'I think my mum might, she might.'

'Know who the little boy was?'

She didn't like the look in his eye.

'Yes.' He came up close to her and the smell was unbreathable. He seemed to be struggling for the right word, or any word. 'Sex,' he said finally. 'I like sex, Nell. Real sex.'

Fortunately his penis wasn't listening.

'Nothing to do with—' He strained for the word and could not find it. Children, she supposed he meant.

He turned away as if she were the one with the putrid smell. Then he whipped back around, noticing her all over again.

'Working, Nell Stone? Typing typing typing, so much to type, so much to say. It must be exhausting being Nell Stone all the time.' He seemed to have struck a vein of words. 'The sound of that fucking machine is the sound of your fucking brain.' He slammed his fist onto the keys. The letters flew up and twisted together. Before she could assess the damage he shoved the typewriter off the desk. It fell on its side. The silver arm snapped off.

He spun and left the house, his movements not his own as he went down the ladder jerkily, as if someone were pulling him with strings. Once in their first month together in the field an Anapa elder had come to her and told her it was not safe for her to be alone with just her husband, and he offered to be her brother. At the time she and Fen had laughed about this. But she had needed a brother, it turned out. She had needed one with the Mumbanyo. She might still have her baby if she'd had a brother there.

She turned off the lamp and tried to sleep. Her heart was beating too fast. She took long breaths but it wouldn't slow. She was scared he'd come back.

She got up and pulled on her filthy clothes. Wanji had not done the laundry since three days before Xambun arrived. There were fewer people on the beach than she had thought, only about fifty, some twenty people dancing and another thirty sprawled out around them. All the dancers were men, beads in their hair like Fen's and special, ceremonial, elaborately curved penis gourds strapped on. The dance was all about these gourds, about making them leap and turn and thrust at the women, who lay about in groups half watching, bemused but sated, like men who'd been in a strip club too long. And there was Fen, in full costume, gyrating, clacking his gourd against his partner's, his movements lacking the fluidity of the others. All the flute players had gone to bed, and the one man with a drum was listing to one side and slapping it only occasionally. A few women chanted or kept time with stones or sticks. Most lay with their heads close together talking, barely watching. Xambun was not there anywhere in the crowd.

The mood Fen had brought up to the house was magnified here. The celebration had turned. The men were tense, doped, some barely upright, others flinging themselves around as if trying to escape their own bodies. There seemed a muted desperation, not the building fury of a Mumbanyo ceremony when she feared they were seconds away from stabbing each other, not homicidal like that but suicidal, as if the women's lack of interest and Xambun's disappearance and the lack of rain were all their fault.

She sat beside a woman named Halana who passed her some kava and taro. She opened her notebook. It was the fifth night. She'd seen it all by now. There was nothing more to add. She heard Boas scolding her: Everything is material, even your own boredom; you never see anything twice—never think you've seen it before because you have not. I am working, she told herself, one of her tricks to re-see, see better, see beyond. Halana stared at her. She imitated Nell holding the pencil, chewing on its end, then pretended to eat the whole thing, which sent her friends into gales of laughter.

The dance went on and on, with no sense of form, of beginning or end. At one point Fen gave her a smile. His anger had passed. She felt herself falling asleep with her eyes open. And then she noticed, off to the left beyond the dancing and close to the water, a flicker of light. She looked hard. It was a tiny orange glow just above the rock that jutted out from the shore. A cigarette? She got up and moved toward it casually, as if she were heading up the path to her house, then she turned into the bushes toward the rock. Through the leaves she could see she was right: it was a cigarette, and hunched over it was the barely discernible shape of a man.

Alone was not something you saw among tribes she'd studied. From an early age children were warned against it. Alone was how your soul got stolen by spirits, or your body kidnapped by enemies. Alone was when your thinking turned to evil. The culture often had proverbs against it. *Not even a possum walks alone* was the Tam's most repeated one. The man on the rock was Xambun, not squatting the way another Tam would be, but sitting, knees drawn up slightly and his torso curled over them, eyes fixed on a point across the water. His body had grown fleshy and pear-shaped from the rice and bully beef they fed mine workers. Shoes were louder than bare feet—he would know it was her—but he did not turn. He lifted the cigarette to his mouth. He was still wearing the mine's green trousers, but no adornments, no beads or bones or shells.

An informant like this in the field, a man who has been raised in the culture but removed for a time so that he is able to see his own people from a different angle with the ability to contrast their behaviors to another set of behaviors, is invaluable. And one who has been exposed to a Western culture—she couldn't think of anyone who had ever accessed that kind of informant in as remote a place.

She wanted to move toward him. She might never get this opportunity again. And yet she felt his need for this solitude. She felt she knew his story already: the child hero, the false promises of the blackbirders, the slavelike treatment at the mine, the perilous escape back here, and the exhaustion of trying to hide it all from his family, to whom he was returning in glory. But she was aware that the story you think you know is never the real one. She wanted his real one. What would he say about it all? She could imagine writing a whole book on him alone.

She hadn't moved but he turned suddenly, looked directly at her, and told her to go away.

It wasn't until she was halfway up her steps that she realized he'd said it not in Tam or in pidgin but in English.

19

3/15 The celebration of Xambun's return does not end. Each morning I think surely they have fished out every fish & shot every fat bird & wild pig, surely they have exhausted their own bodies if not their food supply. And each night I think surely tomorrow everything will return to normal, the women will go out on the lake at sunrise, my morning visitors will come back, the traders will go off trading, but it never happens. They sleep all day because they have been up all night. Just before sunset the drums start up again and the fires get lit and it all goes on for another night: feasting, drinking, dancing, screaming, singing, weeping.

Someone from the next hamlet just returned from the coast having brought several new beach dances. Until now beach dances had been forbidden by the elder generation here but everyone has learned them this week. Given that their standard dance includes swinging the penis hard & fast & imitating copulation with precise & lengthy accuracy, the new dances seem to be as harmless as the Hokey Pokey. The men have painted each other in an intricate design that I haven't seen on their most expensive pottery. Everyone is festooned in their fanciest shells, strings & strings of them, and you have to shout over the din they make.

I have gone through about 50 notebooks in 5 days and yet I feel on the cusp of death by boredom. I know I am a strange bird, fatigued by frenzy, visions, and public fornication. I know as an anthropologist I am supposed to live for these opportunities to see the symbolism of the culture played out. But I don't trust a crowd—hundreds of people together without cognition and only the basest impulses: food, drink, sex. Fen claims that if you just let go of your brain you find another brain, the group brain, the collective brain, and that it is an exhilarating form of human connection that we have lost in our embrace of the individual except when we go to war. Which is my point exactly.

Not to mention my impatience to get to X, to talk to him, to assault him, as Bankson would say. Malun promises she will secure me an interview as soon as the ceremonies are over. She keeps thanking us, and I can't seem to convince her that we had nothing to do with his return.

I wish B hadn't left before X arrived. I could use someone to talk to, someone who is not a mile high on morning glory seeds & something called honi & who knows what else. I have given Tadi a note to give to the Kiona when she goes to market, but she has not gone. No one has left the lake for over a week.

I have come to think of this celebration for Xambun as a wild animal that shifts & eats but might never go away.

20

It was over by the time I got there. I cut my engine and heard no celebrating from any quarter of the village. On the beach crows and buzzards fought for position on the ribs of a wild boar and flies marauded taro skins and fruit rinds nearby. The fire pits were cold, beads and feathers lay half buried in the pounded sand, and the air itself felt exhausted.

The lake was a good bit lower than the last time I was here and the heat had a new density. I dragged my canoe up to the grasses and carried my engine and an extra tank of petrol up the path.

I ran into no one on my way to their house. I recognized the silence, the spent stillness of a village having depleted itself in every way. I wasn't bothered that I had missed the festivities. I was certain Nell had taken impeccable notes. It was the interviewing of Xambun that would yield the most important information.

Out of the opening of one of the men's houses hung a pair of legs, as if the fellow hadn't been able to make it all the way inside before collapsing. It made me aware of my own stores of energy. I felt fitter than I had in a great while, and chuckled at the memory of crashing to the ground the last time I was here. I stashed the engine and petrol below their house and went back down to the beach for the large suitcase I'd brought. At the foot of their ladder I called up softly, not wanting to disturb them if they too were sleeping. No response, so I climbed up. They were both at their typewriters in the large mosquito room.

None of the photographs taken of Nell Stone, the ones you find in textbooks and the two biographies, even the ones taken in the field, ever captured the way she really looked. You cannot see her energy, her quick brimming joy when you came through the door. If I could have any picture of her at all, it would be then, at the moment she saw me that day.

'You came.'

'I'm only staying three months,' I joked, holding up the large case, which seemed even bigger inside the house.

Fen was watching her now, and her face lost its unguarded expression. She gave me a kiss on the cheek, which was over before I could register it. Then she stood back. She smelled somehow like the back garden of Hemsley House, of juniper and laburnum.

'You look quite the gentleman anthropologist. All you need is a—wait! Wait!' She jumped up, flashed out of one mosquito room and into the other, and returned with hat, pipe, and camera. 'Come on. Too dark in here.'

'Nell, he's just arrived for God's sake,' Fen said by way of hello from his chair. He looked awful, blue-black rings under his eyes and his skin papery as an old man's. His shirtfront clung to his chest, sopped in sweat.

'It's a classic,' she said. 'He can put it on the cover of his memoirs.'

She had me go back down the stairs with my suitcase and stand up against the tamarind tree facing their house.

She picked up a long frond from the road and draped it over my shoulder.

'Now bite the pipe.'

I clenched down on it and grimaced, my best imitation of a wizened old master I had at Charterhouse.

'That's it!' But she was laughing too hard to take the photograph.

'Oh Christ, I'll have to do it.'

Fen came down and took three pictures of me. Then we put Nell in the hat with the cases and the pipe and took a few more. A man hurried past us and Fen called after him to borrow his digging stick and heavy necklaces. He handed these items over reluctantly and then looked on with concern as Fen posed with them.

Nell was in full health. From what I could see her lesions had healed, her limp was less pronounced. Her lips were the deep red of a child's. The Tam diet clearly suited her; she was rounder, and her skin looked smooth as soap. The impulse to touch her and all the life in her was something I had to check regularly.

'How are your warriors?' Fen said as we went back up into the house. I recognized it as an idle question, a question posed by someone who was thinking of something else, the way my father might have asked me about school when I came home for a holiday, his mind on a set of cells or tail feathers.

I told them that the Kiona had promised me a Wai.

'Fantastic,' Nell said. 'Can we come?'

'Certainly.' It had been so long since I'd had something to look forward to.

'Party's over here,' Fen said.

'Have you managed to interview him yet?' I said.

'Fen thinks we should play it cool with him, let him come to us.'

'Really?' This surprised me. There was nothing about their style of ethnographic bullying that allowed for 'playing it cool.' They played it hot and fast, and my first thought was to suspect they were lying to me, and I was ashamed of this.

We were inside now, and Fen was pouring us drinks, a fermented cherry juice. He let out a laugh. 'It's not like we have a choice.'

'He told me to go away.'

'We need to give him time,' Fen said. 'He associates us with the mine right now.'

'He needs to talk about it with us, with people who understand what he's been through.'

'Nellie, you don't know what he's been through.'

'Of course I do. He's been an indentured servant to Western greed.'

'Where? Which mine? For how long? He could have been there three months for all we know. And that chap Barton who manages Edie Creek. He's a good sort. I bet he runs a decent operation, if Xambun was there.'

'By my calculations he's been gone over three years. Malun has all her fronds—'

'Her fronds!' Fen turned to me. 'When we first got here she had half the fronds she does now. There is no way to know how long he was gone.'

'Barton is not a good sort. He hosts crocodile parties, Fen.' I didn't know what she meant. 'He bets on the croc and his houseboys die.'

'That's rubbish and you know it. What's in that thing anyway, Bankson? Not sure you even brought a rucksack last time.'

'Minton came by with the post, and he had a few things for the two of you.'

I popped the clasps. I'd put Fen's five letters in the fabric of the side pocket. Nell's post—one hundred and forty-seven pieces of it—filled the rest of the space.

'Schuyler Fenwick.' I handed Fen the thin packet of letters. 'Sorry, mate.'

'No worries. I'm used to it.'

So was she, it appeared. With none of the shock or celebration I had anticipated, she took the suitcase and set about sorting her mountain of correspondence with a businesslike air: family to the left, work to the right, and friends in the middle. She barely paused over any of them, just checked the return address and placed it on a pile. Occasionally a name brought a small smile, but she seemed each time to be hoping for someone else. Fen took his into the workroom and opened them at the desk.

I settled on the sofa and plucked a magazine from Nell's pile. *The New Yorker*, which I'd never seen. On its front was a drawing of tourists at a café in Paris. It was dated August 20, 1932, and the perspective was flattened, with the tables nearly floating in the air, the faces geometric, Picasso-like. Smoke came off a cigarette in a black curlicue. The seven-hour trip in the sun caught up with me and though I meant to open the magazine, my hands were heavy and held it closed. It was a lovely drawing, though perhaps I felt that way because I had not seen a piece of Western art in so long. It filled me with longing, too: the menu, the carafes of wine, the red-and-white checked tablecloths. A waiter came up behind me. He took my order. Squab, I said. Then he turned to Nell, who said squib, and we laughed and I jerked awake.

I worried I'd laughed aloud, but Nell was reading a letter and did not hear me in any case. I could still feel it in my chest and throat, a great bubble of warmth that wanted to escape. Squib and squab. I had a small erection beneath the magazine.

'Bankson!' Fen nudged me. 'I want to show you something.'

I stood woozily and followed him out and down.

'Best to steer clear, really, when she reads all that,' he said.

'Why?'

He shook his head. 'She gets letters now from every crazy person in America. Everyone wants her advice, her approval. Her name on anything is suddenly some magic golden seal. Then there's Helen.'

Fen had stopped below the ceremonial house with the enormous villainous face looming above us, its black prickly snake tongue hanging six feet out of its mouth.

'Who's Helen?'

'Another one of Papa Franz Boas' disciples. Mentally imbalanced. Black, black moods. I had to tell Nell to stop seeing her. Nell writes thirty letters to her one. But she never learns. She always fears the worst. Did you see her pawing through that suitcase for letters from Helen? I don't think there was even one this time.'

But there was a package, I wanted to say. A heavy rectangle with Helen's name and address in the top left corner. 'I'm sorry I brought the post then.'

'Best to get it over with,' he said, and called up to the men inside.

After we climbed up and passed under the mouth of the hideous face, there was a second entrance, narrower than the first, red on both sides. I saw that it was the lower part of another carving, this one of a woman with a shaved head and large breasts that towered above us. Her waist tapered and her legs split and the opening we were about to pass through was her enormous scarlet vulva. Fen stepped through it without remark.

I took my time, examining how it was constructed.

'Look,' he said to me, 'I respect their rules of secrecy. No woman has ever entered this house. So don't tell Nell about anything you see here. It will get her all worked up over nothing.'

The inside of a men's ceremonial house is not all that different to a dining club at Cambridge. There is the same low talk, the same clustering, the same ease. But not for non-members. Even Fen, for whom fitting in seemed the least of concerns, who behaved as if the world should conform to him, walked uncomfortably down the middle of the long room, his eyes adjusting, looking for a man named Kanup. Kanup was the manager of Tam art, the one who decided what would be kept and what would be sold, who set the prices and packed the canoes and oversaw the returns. He had lived with a Kiona woman for a time and as soon as Fen found him Kanup began to speak in great grandiose terms of Tam art and why it was superior to Kiona art and to the art of every other tribe in the region. Kanup was the kind of fellow who wanted your attention and made sure he got it. His Kiona was excellent, and I was compelled as much by his utter bilingualism as I was by his knowledge. I made my notes as I had made all my notes in the field, with full concentration and complete uncertainty as to whether they would be of any use at all. Fen disappeared quickly somewhere in the dim back of the vast room. After a while I was aware of voices escalating into argument behind me. I worried it was my presence in their house that was causing the trouble, but when I was able to break away from Kanup's steady stare on me, I saw their focus was at the back of the room, in the dark alcove where Fen was. I could not see what he was doing or whom he was with.

'What was going on back there?' I asked him on the path home.

'Nothing.'

'What were you doing?'

'Nothing. Resting. Waiting for you.' But he was lying, and not going to great pains to hide it.

21

When we returned to the house the lamps were lit and Nell was on the floor in a circle of open letters, a large calendar on her lap.

Fen flopped on the sofa behind her. 'Get your Nobel Prize yet, Nellie?'

'Stalin's wife has died mysteriously, and John Layard has taken up with Doris Dingwall!'

"I thought he was in Berlin with the poets,' I said, taking a chair in the corner.

'Apparently he got very depressed, bungled a suicide attempt, then went to Auden's flat to get him to finish him off. Leonie says Auden was sorely tempted, but he ended up taking him to the hospital. Then he flew back to England where he's stolen Doris from Eric.'

Doris and Eric Dingwall were anthropologists at University College in London—and known for their open marriage.

'What are we doing in November?' she asked Fen.

'Buggered if I know. Why?'

'They've asked me to give the keynote at the International Congress.' She was trying to keep her voice modulated for Fen's sake.

'That's fantastic!' I said, trying on some American enthusiasm. 'Quite an honor.'

'And they've asked me to be an assistant curator at the museum. They're going to give me an office in the turret.'

'Good onya, Nellie. How's our bank account?'

She gave him a cautious smile. 'Very healthy.'

'Is this what I think it is?' Fen said. He tapped Helen's package on the floor with his toe. 'You haven't opened it.'

'No.'

Fen looked at me sharply, as if I knew what that meant. I did not.

'Come on, Nellie.' He bent down and put it in her lap. 'Let's have a look. Plus we could use this.' He plucked at the heavy grey twine it was wrapped up in.

Beneath the brown post paper was a box. Inside the box was a slim manuscript, not more than three hundred pages. Its pages were flat, its edges perfectly aligned. We stood in slight awe of it, as if it might speak or burst into flames. Nell had already done this, taken her hundreds of notebooks and magically compressed them into a stack of clean, unbuckled sheets of paper, taken millions of details and slotted them into some sort of order to make a book, but Fen and I had not. From this vantage point that transformation seemed impossible.

On top of the stack was a note in small thick writing.

Dear Nell,

    Finally. Hope you and Fen will have time to take a look. No enormous hurry. Am giving it to Papa today and I'm sure he'll have me revising through the summer. If Fen has trouble with my presentation of the Dobu he needs to tell

me honestly and unsparingly. I just received
your first letter with the Mumbanyo. They sound
appalling. I'm sure you've tamed them by now.
All love,
H

They both looked at this note for a long while, as long as it would take to read a full page of writing. The silence was not still—it was the opposite of stillness. As if the three of them, Nell, Fen, and Helen, were having a conversation I couldn't hear.

'Shall we have a look?' I said. 'I'll make the tea'.

'Teatime!' Fen said in the voice of a Cambridge tea lady. 'Make haste!'

'All of us read it? Together?' Nell said, coming out of her trance.

'Why not?'

I was hungry for it. I ached for a new idea, a new thought in my head. I made the tea quickly, scooting around Bani as unobtrusively as I could in that small corner of the house.

Nell began reading as soon as I set the pot and cups down on the trunk. On the first pages Helen declared Western civilization's lack of understanding of other peoples' customs to be the world's greatest and gravest social problem. By page twenty she had brought in Copernicus, Dewey, Darwin, Rousseau, and Linnaeus' *Homo ferus,* swept around the globe a few times, and asserted that the notion of racial heredity, of a pure race, is bunk, that culture is not biologically transmitted, and that Western civilization is not the end result of an evolution of culture, nor is the study of primitive societies the study of our origins.

In this first chapter she had laid down in simple honest language many of the tenets our generation of anthropologists felt but had never put on the page so clearly. But it was impossible to stop there. We took turns reading. We devoured her words. It felt as if she had written the book for us and only us, a fat message that said: Carry on. You can do this. This is important. You are not wasting your time.

The most intoxicating drug could not have had a stronger effect on me. A few chapters in and Bani was standing over us, speaking loudly. Apparently he'd been trying to tell us dinner was ready. We took the book with us to the table which had been set with linens and platters of food. Fen took over the reading, managing bites between sentences, and I supposed we didn't appreciate the meal sufficiently, for Bani left without saying goodbye or doing the washing up.

Fen read on, standing up in the little kitchen area, while Nell and I cleaned the dishes. When he got to the part about where Helen accuses Malinowski of treating his Trobriands as generic primitives, he fairly screamed it. And then he looked up from the page, eyes ablaze. 'Is it my imagination or did she just take down Frazer, Spengler, *and* Malinowski in those three pages?'

We laughed all three as one loud person. We were giddy with her iconoclasm, her courage, her ambition. Fen read on. Primitive societies, she allowed, were easier to study than our more complex Western civilization, much like the beetle was easier for Darwin when establishing his theories than the human being.

'Rot!' Nell yelled at the page. 'We've had that beetle argument a million times. And I always win. But she puts that in there anyway.' She pulled a short pencil out from somewhere in her hair and made to cross out the last sentences.

'Hey ho,' Fen said, blocking her. 'Let her have her full say before you start blanking it all out.'

We moved back to the sofa and I brought out a jug of Kiona 'wine' that tasted like sweetened rubber. Fen passed the manuscript to me and I began reading. This section was about the Zuni of New Mexico, who carved out an existence and an 'attitude towards existence' that was completely at odds with the rest of the tribes of North America, who often used drugs and fermented cactus juice to 'get religious.'

'I'm feeling a bit religious myself,' Fen said. 'This wretched stuff is potent.'

Nell didn't say anything—she was scribbling notes on a pad—but her cup was half empty and her cheeks blazed. The top of her pencil was wet and chewed.

Other tribes danced until their mouths frothed or they had seizures or visions, but the Zuni simply danced to methodically alter nature. 'The tireless pounding of their feet draws together the mist in the sky and heaps it into the piled rain clouds. It forces out the rain upon the earth.'

Nell was nodding as I read. 'Beautiful,' she said.

'Terrible!' Fen hopped to his feet, pointing at the page. 'That's it right there. That's the line she can't cross. She loses all her authority right there.'

'She is bringing us into the moment,' Nell said. 'Into the heart of the culture.'

'It's a fake. She knows full well the pounding of the feet doesn't bring the rain.'

'Of course, Fen. But she is capturing right there how the Zuni see it, telling it from their point of view.'

'That's just sloppy. It's catering to a mass audience and not the scholar. She's too good to make that mistake.'

This last shut Nell up.

'What do you think, Bankson?' Fen said. 'Yes or no on the rain being forced from the earth? Is the good scientist allowed artistic license?'

I chose to continue reading. It was the Dobu section. Fen was the only anthropologist to have ever studied the Dobu, so Helen's entire portrait of the culture came from his monograph published in *Oceania* and a series of interviews she conducted with him in New York. I braced myself for Fen's protests, but he cheered Helen on as she plunged into a disturbing description of a lawless society whose chief virtues were ill will and treachery. Instead of an open communal dance plaza, the center of the village was a graveyard. Instead of communal gardens, each family planted its own yams on rocky private terrain and relied on magic and magic alone for their growth, believing that the yam tubers wandered at night below the ground and only charms and countercharms would entice them home—that the growth of one's garden depended solely on magic, and not on the amount of seeds one planted.

'That cannot be true,' Nell said, slapping the page.

'Are you doubting your dear friend Helen or your beloved husband or both?'

'This wasn't in your monograph. Did you tell her this?'

'Of course I did.'

175

'And you honestly believe that the Dobu did not see a correlation between number of seeds and number of crops?'

'That is correct.'

I hurried on. Because there was never enough food and they were often half starving, the Dobu had developed a great many superstitions around cultivation. They also felt that the yams didn't like playing, singing, laughing, or any form of happiness, but that having sex in the garden was essential for growth. Wives were always blamed for the death of their spouse, and it was believed that women could leave their sleeping bodies and do deadly deeds, and as a result, women were deeply feared. They were also deeply desired, and no woman without a chaperone was safe from male advances. They were prudish and reluctant to discuss sex, but they had a lot of it and reported great satisfaction. Mutual sexual satisfaction was important to the Dobu. I could feel my skin burning as I read. Fortunately Fen was concentrating on Helen's words too closely to tease me about it. One of their most important spells was the spell of invisibility, used primarily for thieving and adultery.

'They taught me that one,' Fen said. 'I still know it by heart. Come in handy someday.'

'"The Dobuan," Helen concluded, "lives out without repression man's worst nightmares of the ill-will of the universe."'

'I think they're the most terrifying people I've ever read about,' I said.

'Fen was a little unstable when I met him,' Nell said. 'His eyes were like this.' She stretched her eyelids as open as possible.

'I'd been frightened out of my mind every day for two years,' he said.

'I wouldn't have lasted half that,' I said, but it occurred to me that the Dobu sounded a lot like him: his paranoid streak, his dark humor, his distrust of pleasure, his secrecy. I couldn't help questioning the research. When only one person is the expert on a particular people, do we learn more about the people or the anthropologist when we read the analysis? As usual, I found myself more interested in that intersection than anything else.

At some point Fen brought out cans of sardines and apricots that we ate with our fingers, our stomachs suddenly as ravenous as our minds. We all had our notebooks out by then, making notes for Helen and notes for ourselves, and everything got stained as we tried to read and write and argue and eat all at the same time.

Looking at our faces you might have said we were all feverish and half mad, and perhaps you would have been right, but Helen's book made us feel we could rip the stars from the sky and write the world anew. For the first time I saw how I might write a book about the Kiona. I even made a small outline of how it might be shaped. And just these few words in my notebook made many things feel possible.

There was a pale violet light in the sky when Fen read the last pages, Helen's final push toward the understanding that every culture has its own unique goals and orients its society in the direction of those goals. She described the whole set of human potentialities as a great arc, and each culture a selection of traits from that arc. These last pages reminded me of the finale of a fireworks show, many flares sent up at once, exploding one after the other. She claimed that because of the emphasis in the West on private property, our freedom was restricted much more than in many primitive societies. She said that it was often taboo in a culture to have a real discussion of the dominant traits; in our culture, for example, a real discussion of capitalism or war was not permitted, suggesting that these dominant traits had become compulsive and overgrown. Homosexuality and trance were considered abnormalities now, while in the Middle Ages people had been made saints for their trances, which were considered the highest state of being, and in Ancient Greece, as Plato makes clear, homosexuality was 'a major means to the good life.' She claimed that conformity created maladjustment and tradition could turn psychopathic. Her last sentences urged acceptance of cultural relativism and tolerance of differences.

'Written by a true deviant,' Fen said, tossing the last page down. 'A true paranoid deviant. She gets a little hysterical at the end there, as if the whole world's just about to go down the gurgler.'

Nell caught me looking at her. 'What?'

'You look like you are trying to follow about nine different strands of thought.'

'More like forty-three. We should go to bed before our heads explode.' She went down the ladder to drape a banana leaf across the bottom rung, which discouraged visitors. 'All right. We are closed for business until further notice.'

Fen drained the last of the rubber wine into his mouth. It dribbled down his chin and he wiped it with the back of his hand. He took off his shirt, scrubbed his armpits with it, and tossed it in a pile for Wanji.

'To Bedfordshire, my lady,' he said in my accent, taking her arm as they moved to their room. 'Nighty-nighty.'

I went off to my mat in their study feeling a bit like the family pet who'd been put outside for the night. I lay awake as the animals woke up first, snapping branches and blundering through leaves and hollering out, then the humans, coughing, grunting, whining, shouting. Cackles from the women going down to their canoes and their paddling and their songs that carried across the water. Gongs and scoldings and laughter, the thunk of gulls into the water and flying foxes smashing into trees. Finally, I fell asleep. I dreamt I was on an ice floe, squatting like a native, carving a large symbol into the ice. But it was melting, and though I carved deeply—something with two lines crossed in the middle, a glyph representative of whole paragraphs of thought—the ice was turning to slush, and my feet slipped into the sea.

I woke up to the sound of writing, the scrape of the pencil and the softer susurrations of the hand following along. I rolled over, expecting to see Nell at the kitchen table, but it was Fen. He didn't stop. He didn't see me watching. He bent close to the paper and his face was contorted in concentration, and he held his breath for far too long then released it through his nose loudly. If I hadn't known better, I would have said he was sitting on the loo. When there was stirring in the bedroom, he stopped, gathered his pages, and left the house with them.

Nell came out wearing what she must have slept in, large cotton pants and a light green shirt. She fixed us tall mugs of coffee with evaporated milk, and sat where Fen had been. I didn't know if it was ten in the morning or four in the afternoon. Light came through in slits and spackles from no particular direction. I felt like a boy on holiday from school. She sat with both feet up on her seat, her mug on one knee. I sat across from her, Helen's transcript between us.

She bent one corner of the pages with her thumb then let them tick slowly back into place. 'She was always writing a book, but after a while, I began to assume she'd never finish it. I thought I'd moved past her in that way. And now—this makes mine look like a child's scrapbook of souvenirs from a trip to Cincinnati. She's done some head-splitting thinking here. While I've been collecting pretty little stones, she's built a whole cathedral.'

I still felt the tension of the dream in my body, the symbol I was trying to etch in the softening ice. It struck me as funny that she aspired to create a cathedral and I had struggled to carve out one symbol.

'You're laughing at me and my pity party.'

'No.' I thought of the story she told me about running out of spit in the closet. I could see that four-year-old so clearly now.

'Yes, you are.'

'No, I'm not,' but I couldn't stop smiling. 'I feel the same way.'

'No you don't. Look at you. You're all rangy and relaxed, with a big grin on your face.'

'I think Fen might have begun his cathedral this morning.'

'Writing?'

'Pages and pages.'

She seemed surprised, but unimpressed. 'He chases down these things that are nothing in the end. And now Xambun is here and he won't help me with him. I can't enter a men's house. The more fuss I make about it, the more he

resists, and we could leave here in five months without ever
having interviewed him.'

'I could try to have a word—'

'No, please don't. He'd know we'd spoken and it would
make it worse.'

I wanted to help her, offer her something. I told her
about the second entryway of the men's house I'd seen the
day before, as delicately as I could.

'You're saying you walk through her *labia*?' she said,
already reaching for her notebook. 'This is the kind of thing
he's deliberately keeping from me.'

'Perhaps he's respecting their taboos.'

'Fen doesn't give a damn about taboos. Nor should he.
We're trying to piece this culture together, and I've got a partner who withholds information.'

She sharpened a pencil and made me tell her again, in
greater detail. She asked many, many questions, which led
to a discussion about the vulva and the way various tribes on
the Sepik used the image. In the end I did feel I'd given her if
not a conversation with Xambun, then something she could
use. It turned her mood around, and I felt how exhilarating
it would be to work in the field with this woman. Our conversation veered back to the manuscript on the table. We read
through the first chapter again, making notes in the margins.
We rewrote the opening and went into the study, where she
could type it up. The desks were side by side and I read what
we'd written aloud as she typed. We moved onto the next
chapter, both of us reading along silently now, stopping at
certain passages, often the same passages, and making a note
for Helen. Several children had ignored the big banana leaf

over the ladder and climbed up into the house anyway. They sat outside the mosquito netting watching us, occasionally attempting to imitate the strange sounds we made.

Fen returned in time for the Dobu chapter. He didn't like what he saw, the two of us alone together, working on Helen's book, and he sulked until Nell got him to tell the story about the Dobu man who was convinced his invisibility charm was working perfectly and snuck into women's houses only to be struck with a digging stick at the door every time. Then he described the love hex a healer had put on him the day before he left. There was no question that he believed it to be wholly responsible for how quickly he fell in love with Nell on the boat home.

Nell went off on her rounds and Fen and I caught the last bit of a scarification in a ceremonial house. The initiate, a boy of no more than twelve, was wailing and a group of older boys were holding him down on a log while a few men cut into him, making hundreds of small slits on his back and shoulders. They dropped a citrus mixture into each wound so that the skin would puff up and the scars would be raised and textured to look like crocodile skin. His blood had soaked the log in dark striations. When they were done they painted him with oil and turmeric and smeared him with white clay and carried him off weeping and half conscious into seclusion until he healed.

Fen and I walked down to the beach. I'd seen dozens of scarifications but it didn't get easier to watch. My legs felt spongy and my chest burned. We sat in the sand and I don't know that we exchanged a word.

That evening we gathered for the blessing of the food storage huts, which were nearly empty after all the festivities for Xambun. We were all crowded into the small area around the food sheds, but no one stood within five feet of me or Fen, whereas Nell had a little girl in her arms, another child on her back, and several children encircling her legs. Adults wore the totemic plants of their clan. A pair of yams were carried into each shed and blessed and urged to procreate. Ancestors were invoked in long songs and prayers. I was hot and tired of standing and still queasy from the scarification. Somewhere in the bush was that boy in a small hut alone, weeping and blind with pain.

Fen nudged me and I followed his gaze to a man at the edge of the crowd. Even if I hadn't known about him, I would have said he was different. People stood near him, men his age and a girl quite close, but he looked more alone, more psychically removed, than any native I'd ever seen. At the end of the ceremony he was called up to stand at the door of a storage house, but he wouldn't move. The crowd urged him up, but eventually a garland of tubers was brought to him and placed around his neck. He lifted his head briefly. It seemed all he could do to not rip the heavy necklace off. He was meant to sing the final prayer but he did not, and after a few moments Malun came forward and did it for him.

We talked about him on the way back to the house. Nell agreed with me about his disposition but Fen thought we were overreacting. To him Xambun seemed like any young man returned home after being away for a long time: mildly disoriented, figuring out his new path. Nell wanted to start interviewing him straightaway. She wanted Fen to go find him in one of the men's houses, but Fen persuaded her that Xambun needed a few more days to settle in, that they would get better information once he got back in the rhythm of his old life.

22

I have a biographer now, a young fellow who comes round wearing untucked shirts and thick specs. My mother makes him tea and he proceeds to ask me questions. This is the one he seems to want to get at most, the question he brings back visit after visit, sometimes saving it for last, or putting it right up front, or burying it in the middle, thinking he might trip me up. How did you come up with the Grid? I have thought a great deal about why I do not answer. Partly it is shame—though that word hardly captures the depth of it—that prevents me from responding. Another part is that our innocence, our utter ignorance of what lay ahead for Germany and the world, is now nearly impossible to comprehend. And another part still wonders: If we had not come up with the Grid, had not had that experience together, and if I had not stayed but gone back to the Kiona, would any of the rest have happened?

It was late on that third night of my stay on Lake Tam that it happened, that shift in all our stars.

We were back at the kitchen table. We'd gone through Helen's book again, filled it with marginalia in three different hands.

'I keep thinking there's a way to map all of it,' Nell said. I'd seen how her notes were filled with sketches and diagrams.

'What do you mean?' But I knew, of course. I'd seen it. I'd dreamt it.

'Map the arc?' Fen said.

'Orientation.' She and I said it at the same time, that one word. *Orientation.*

'The idea that cultures have a strong pull in one direction, at the expense of other directions.'

I was drawing the first line as she spoke.

At the expense of other directions. I felt like her words were pulling it out of me and at the same time my axis was pulling the words out of her. I wasn't sure if I was having my own thoughts or hers. And yet I felt the melting ice, the sense of urgency. I bisected the line. Just as I had drawn it in my dream.

Fen, somehow understanding completely, pointed to the top of the page, above the top of the vertical line. 'Mumbanyo.' And then to the bottom of it. 'Anapa.'

We fell on this piece of paper, each of us with our pencils, shouting out and filling in the four points of the compass with the names of tribes and then countries. If we stopped at that moment and suggested criteria, defined each direction of the compass, I have no recollection of it. In my memory we went at it instinctively, fully agreeing that Americans were Northerners like the Mumbanyo and that Italians belonged in the South with the Anapa. To the West were the Zuni and to the East the Dobu and the other Dionysian North American tribes. We had to add Southeast for the Baining and Northeast for the Kiona. We ran out of room and had to add a page to all four sides of the initial paper, sticking them together with fig sap and then racing on to get our ideas on the page. We were all bent close together, arms overlapping, foul-breathed and two-years filthy, and I felt like I was back in England with my brothers, included in some pressing project of theirs, making a birdhouse or the backdrop to one of Martin's elaborate plays.

In time we did work out definitions for each point of our compass. The cultures we put in the Northern vector were aggressive, possessive, forceful, successful, ambitious, egoistic. The id of the grid, Nell said. By contrast the Southern cultures were responsive, nurturing, sensitive, empathetic, war-averse. To the West were the Apollonian managers who valued unemotional efficiency, pragmatism, extroversion, while the Easterners were spiritual, introverted seekers, interested in the questions of life more than the answers.

Fen's own temperament did not allow him to dissolve indefinitely into our collective thinking; he participated awhile then pushed us away, as if gasping for breath. When Nell tried to align one of Jung's functions of consciousness to each quadrant, Fen slapped her pencil away from the page.

'You don't understand a thing about it.'

'Explain it to me then.'

'It's far more complex than what you've got here. There are sixteen combinations of dominance.'

She flipped over to a fresh page in her notebook. 'What are they?'

But he wouldn't tell her.

'You haven't put in the Tam,' I said, thinking to smooth over the tension.

'Go ahead,' Nell said to him.

He shook his head.

'Fen. Go on.'

The omission had been deliberate.

186

'What does it matter what my opinion is? Yours is the one that counts.'

'What are you talking about?'

'I'm talking about'—he wrapped both fists around his pencil—'I'm talking about the charade of us doing this to-gether when we both know what you think about the Tam is what people are going to know about the Tam.' He turned to me. 'She thinks she knows the Tam men. She thinks they're vain and gossipy like Western women. She thinks she's found this big swap of sexual roles but she doesn't spend any time with men. She's not making canoes and building houses with them as I am. She doesn't give a tinker's cuss for my notes.'

'You *have* no notes! You've given me next to nothing.'

'Eighteen pages in one day on cross-sexual kinship lines.'

'Which turned out to be based on a false premise.' She looked down at our paper and took in a steadying breath. 'You will write your own book, Fen. You will write what you see and—'

'And who will read that? Who will read *that* when there's a book by *Nell Stone* on the same subject?' He flung the pencil across the house. 'Fucked if I do, fucked if I don't,' he said, slumped in his chair.

'You are certainly fucked if you don't do the work we're here for. And I'm fucked, too.' Nell slammed his pencil back on the table. 'You put down the Tam men and I'll put down the Tam women.'

She waited for him to go first. It took a while, an awk-ward silent while, but then he lifted himself and put the Tam men in the aggressive but artistic Northeast. She put the Tam women in the Northwest.

187

And this led to another round of mapping as we separated men from women, finding that while the male ethos usually represented the culture at large, within a culture women offset the ideal.

'Sort of a built-in thermostat,' Nell said.

Fen tried to resist, to continue to sulk, but he was as compelled by the idea as we were. We talked of women we knew, the way they worked against the aggressive Western male norms. The hours passed. Sometime before dawn the sky rumbled and we went outside to see if this was it, the beginning of the real rains, but it wasn't. The heat was heavy and wet and we decided a swim before sleep might do us good.

As we were stumbling back up the path from the beach, one of us said, 'Could it work for individuals?'

And we raced the rest of the way back, scrambled to make another grid. I still have that old page, wrinkled from the lake water that dripped from our hair.

NORTH
strong-willed
possessive
aggressive
achievement-oriented
competetive
assertive

WEST
pragmatic
managerial
linear
organized
black/white, no grey
systematic
external

EAST
creative
artistic
spiritual
internal
all grey
nonconformist
internal

SOUTH
caring
responsive
flexible
compassionate
yielding
compliant

It was easy to slot people in. We started with famous strong personalities: dreamy, spritelike Nijinsky in the East and the punishing, cane-carrying Diaghilev in the West; Hoover in the North and Edna St. Vincent Millay in the South. We added colleagues, friends, relatives. While Fen and Nell were arguing about whether someone named Leonie was Northeastern or just Eastern, I put Martin beside Helen in the East, and John next to Nell's mother at Northwest. But Nell caught me.

'And your mother?' she said.

'Northern to the bone.'

She laughed, as if she has suspected as much.

'What are we then? Fen said. 'We have to put ourselves on here.'

'You're Northern, I'm Southern and Bankson's Southern.'

'Oh, that's cozy,' Fen said.

'Should I feel insulted?' I said quickly, hoping to diffuse it.

'Hardly,' he said, pointing to the South. 'To be Southern is to be perfect in Nell's mind. Look who's there with you: Boas, her grandmother, and her baby sister who died before ever speaking a word.'

'Stop it, Fen.'

'Sorry I'm not a sensitive little prat who can pick up on your every thought and tend to every nick and bug bite.'

'This is not about us, Fen.'

'The hell it isn't.'

'Let's just stick to—' Nell said, but a frantic crunch and rustle through the thatch above us drowned her out. Rats fleeing something.

'Snake,' Fen said.

It slipped fast down a post and was gone.

'I hate snakes,' I said. In fact my stomach had soured just from the sound of it.

'So do I,' she said.

'Bloody Southern cowards," Fen said.

And we were all right for a while after that.

We kept at it. The sun came up and went down again. We believed we were in the throes of a big theory. We could see our grid in chalk on university blackboards. It felt like we were putting a messy disorganized unlabeled world in order. It felt like decoding. It felt like liberation. Nell and I spoke of never having felt aligned with our culture, with its values and expectations. For long stretches of time it felt like we were crawling around in each other's brain. We talked in the abstract about relationships, which temperaments went well together. Nell said opposites worked best, and I hastened to agree, though I didn't believe it, and hoped she didn't either. She said that Southerners were less possessive with their lovers, more inclined to polygamy.

'It's what her set calls free love,' Fen said. 'Multiple partners. You go in for that too, Bankson?'

'No.' It was the only answer I could give him under the circumstances.

'Well then, a possessive Southerner for you,' he said to Nell.

Later, when Fen went to the shit house, as he called it, she said, 'Do you think it's natural, the desire to possess another person?'

'Natural? Weren't you the one to warn me off that word?' When Fen was there I was able to contain my attraction to her, but whenever he left I felt it fill the room.

She smiled, but she was serious. 'Instinctive then, bio-logical? Why are there so many tribes who share everything— food, shelter, land, income—but their stories always revolve around someone's brother or best friend stealing his woman?'

'It's true. The Kiona's creation myth is about a crocodile who falls in love with his brother's wife and they run off to-gether to create a new tribe.'

'Have you ever felt that, the impulse to possess someone?'

'Yes.' But I could hardly tell her how recently. 'Perhaps I'm not so Southern after all.' Then, to deflect her, I told her about Sophie Soules, a French girl I was engaged to briefly the summer after Martin died, and that when I broke it off, her father had me write a letter attesting to her virginity.

'A letter promising you had not possessed her. Was it the truth?'

She *was* a nosy parker. 'Of course,' I paused, 'it was not true.'

She laughed. 'Was she wine or bread to you?'

'What do you mean?'

'It's from an Amy Lowell poem we all loved in college. Wine is sort of thrilling and sensual, and bread is familiar and essential.'

'Wine, I suppose.'

'Would it have turned to bread?'

'I don't know.'

'It doesn't always.'

'No, I suppose not.'

She rolled a pencil beneath her palm on the table and then she looked up at me. 'Helen and I were lovers,' she said.

'Ah.' This explained a few things.

She laughed at my 'ah' and told me they had met during Nell's first anthropology class with Boas. Helen, a decade older, was his graduate assistant. Their connection was instant and though Helen was married with a house in White Plains, she stayed in the city many nights a week. She had encouraged Nell to go and study the Kirakira, but wrote her angry letters accusing Nell of abandoning her. Then she surprised her by meeting the boat in Marseille with the news that she had left her husband.

'But you had met Fen.'

'I had met Fen. And it was awful. Before Helen, I would have said that the desire to possess others is more male than female in our culture, but I think temperament comes into it.' She tapped the pencil on our Grid.

'Was she bread to you?'

She shook her head slowly. 'People are always wine to me, never bread.'

'Maybe that's why you don't want to possess them.'

Fen didn't come back for over an hour, and when he did his face was ruddy and bright, as if he'd been out in the cold. Neither of us asked him where he'd been. We continued to work on the Grid until Fen looked up and said, 'I wonder what the baby will be.'

'Fen.'

'What baby?' I said.

'Our baby,' he said. He leaned back, deeply satisfied by my shock.

It all felt very unpleasant to me and I couldn't look at either of them, nor think of a single word to say.

'You haven't told him then, Nellie? Didn't want him to fuss about?'

Is that how she saw me, as someone who fretted over her unnecessarily? Is that what a 'Southern' man signified to her? Finally I eked out some sort of congratulations, said, 'Excuse me,' and got out of the house.

I walked down the men's road. A cluster of pigs were muscling each other for a scrap of food beneath one of the houses and making a racket. There was very little light in the sky, but whether it was sunrise or dusk, I wasn't sure anymore. I had been spun around by them. I was seven hours away from my work, and had been for who knew how many days. Nell was pregnant. She and Fen had made a baby. When I was with them it was easy to convince myself that she hadn't fully made her choice yet. She played her part in that. Her eyes burned into mine when I had an idea she liked. She followed every word I said; she referred back. When I had written down Martin's name on the graph she'd passed her finger over the letters. I felt in some ways we'd had some sort of sex, sex of the mind, sex of ideas, sex of words, hundreds and thousands of words, while Fen slept or shat or disappeared. But his kind of sex with her produced a baby. Mine was useless.

Where the houses ended the road broke in three directions: straight to the next hamlet, left toward the water, and right to the women's road. At this intersection up ahead, I saw two shapes against the trees, a man and a woman. They were not touching. If I hadn't known better I would have said the man was white, not because of his skin color, which I could not see in the nearly complete darkness, but in the way he stood sloped and heavy with his weight out in front. As I got closer I could hear they were arguing, the girl in a pleading tone, and when the man saw me he started toward me, then stopped short. He turned back and said something to the girl and they moved on quickly up the women's road. Xambun. It had been Xambun. And for those few steps he'd taken toward me, he'd thought I was Fen.

I went down to the beach. It was empty, the water unnaturally far away. The canoes were lined up, mine included, high up the beach. Fen's pews. Had he begun interviewing Xambun without telling Nell? I paced for a while, then stood in one place too long and something crawled up the inside of my trouser leg and I shook it out. Scorpion. I stepped on it heavily and the crunch of its carapace and brittle bones was deeply satisfying. I moved quickly up the sand, back to the house. Their lamps were still lit. I put my hands on the ladder and heard their voices. I moved under the house to hear them more clearly.

'I can see it, Nell. I can see it right in front of me and I can hear it in your voice and I can feel it under my skin. I'm not inventing anything.'

'This is what you do. That's why you're a Northerner. You want to keep people under lock and key. One real conversation with someone else and—'

'Oh,' he began in falsetto, 'you're a Southerner and I'm a Southerner and he's an asshole. I recognize this. That was *me* three years ago. And now I'm Helen on the fucking quai.'

'You're extrapolating all—'

'That's right. I am *extrapolating*, Nell. And brilliantly, like the trained scientist that I am. This whole thing is a way for the two of you to *screw* right in front of me.'

'That is ridiculous and you know it.'

'I will *never* be one of your castoffs, Nellie.'

'Don't.'

'I'm not—'

'I mean it.'

'Goddamn it, Nell.'

When I came in, Nell was straightening up our grid papers. She didn't look at me.

'There you are,' Fen said.

'I'm going to get some shut-eye,' Nell said.

I ached for sleep as well, but wanted to keep him from lying down beside her for as long as possible. I poured us each a drink and took the sofa, which faced their bedroom. Nell brought a lamp with her, wrote something briefly on her bed, and blew out the light. Fen watched me watch her. It was too dark to see anything, but I knew her already, knew her breasts and the narrow of her back, the rise of her bum and the knot of her calf. I knew the break in her ankle and scars on her skin and her short round toes.

He told me about a letter he'd gotten from a friend in Northern Rhodesia. The friend had told him a story about his shoes being stolen and the village-wide hunt for them. It was a long story with the shoes ending up in the trunk of an elephant, and Fen told it badly.

'That's funny,' I said.

'It's absurd,' he said. But neither of us was laughing.

When he stood to go to bed, I told him I'd be gone in the morning. In fact, I thought I'd leave after they were asleep. She would be safer, I concluded, if I were not around to enrage him.

He sat back down. 'No. No. You can't *go*.'

'Why not?'

'I need you here. We both need you here. We need to keep going with this theory.'

'You don't need me for that. It's not my area, personality typing.'

'I can't explain it all right now.' He lowered his voice and glanced to her bedroom, 'But you have to stay. I'm sorry. I've been . . .' He dipped his head into his hands and raked his fingernails through his hair loudly. 'I've been awful. I'm stretched a little thin right now. Stay just one more day. A half day. Leave tomorrow afternoon. Please.'

And stupidly, selfishly, I agreed.

23

3/21 Brain ablaze. Feel like we are unearthing something and finding ourselves, knowing ourselves, stripping off layers of our upbringing like old paint. Can't write about it fully yet. Don't understand it. I only know that when F leaves and B and I talk I feel like I am saying—and hearing—the first wholly honest words of my life.

24

I awoke to sobbing. Nell. In pain. I got up off my mat and pushed through the netting. I found her sitting on the floor at the front of the house, a girl shaking and howling in her arms. It was the girl from the night before, the one arguing with Xambun. Nell smiled at me in my underwear, but the girl kept up her crying. I retreated to my room. The girl saved enough breath for a few words and Nell cooed something back to her. Tatem mo shilai, it sounded like. He will come back. After a long while they stood and Nell wiped the girl's face and led her out and down the ladder. I had got on my trousers and shirt by the time she returned.

'There's been a good deal of drama this morning.' She said something to Bani, whom I hadn't seen behind the kitchen screen.

'Tell me.' I came through the netting and sat at the table with her. She was wearing the pale green shirt again, now streaked with the girl's tears.

Bani brought out coffee. I thanked him and he smiled and said something to Nell.

'He says you speak like his Kiona cousins.' Then she slid a piece of paper toward me.

```
Bankson—
    I know you wanted to get back, but what's
another few days in paradise, right? It's now
```

or never. Don't be miffed I didn't invite you
along. Someone needs to stay with Nell and
you're clearly the Southern man for the job.

'He's taken your canoe,' she said. 'That was Umi, Xambun's girl. He's broken it off with her, told her he was going
to go away soon. Move to Australia. And now he's gone with
Fen. This whole time—all those times Fen kept leaving the
house—he was scheming with Xambun. Not even interviewing him, just plotting to get that goddamn flute.'

I thought of the way he kept disappearing, the way his
moods shifted, the way his attention slipped in and out. The
way Xambun had moved toward me the night before, expec-
tantly, then shrunk back when he saw I wasn't Fen.

'I'm such a dope not to have seen this coming,' she said.
'He's been lying to me for weeks.'

What had he told me? That he knew the route, that it
would change the next moon. That he would go in upriver
of the village. No one would hear him. No one would know.
I'd underestimated him entirely. I'd thought his inertia was
permanent, that he luxuriated in his sense of missed opportunity and bad luck.

'He's promised Xambun money, I'm sure,' she said.
'Money to move to Australia.'

Without an engine it would take more than a day to
catch up to them. Maybe I could find a pinnace to take me to
the Mumbanyo. I stood. 'I'll get some men. We'll find a way
to stop them.'

'At this point you'll only give them away, make it worse.'

I remained in place, indecisive, weak.

'Stay here. Please.'

They were hours ahead of me. This was the only time I would have with her alone. I sat back down.

'Are you worried for his safety?' I said.

'He took his gun. I'm more worried for theirs.'

'Won't they follow him back up here?'

'If they see him, they might. But there are other tribes I think they'd suspect first. The Mumbanyo have a lot of enemies.' She crushed the note in her hand. 'Damn him.'

Five or six heads of children appeared at the bottom of the doorway, halfway up the steps, ready to climb up the rest at the slightest invitation.

She looked at them longingly. They were what made sense to her.

'Let's get back to work,' I said.

She waved the children in.

I spent the rest of the morning observing the observer. She was back in her element, cross-legged on the floor with a circle of children fanned out around her and three more squished in her lap. They played a clapping game in which you keep a rhythm and have to shout out in turn some sort of response. She was able to keep the beat against her thigh with her left hand while taking notes with her right and shout out an answer in Tam when it was her turn. When the littlest girl called out her answer everyone collapsed on the ground with laughter. Nell didn't understand, and once an older boy had gotten control of himself he explained it and Nell let out a big laugh and they all collapsed again.

After a while she moved on to another group, and then another. Somehow they all knew they had to wait their turn for her attention—there was no interrupting her when she was with another group. Bani brought in snacks throughout the morning so the energy remained high. I watched all this from my chair at the table until, after a conversation with an old man, Nell called me over and asked if I'd heard of something called a bolunta. I hadn't. She said it sounded a bit like a Wai. And this man, Chanta, had seen it once. His mother was Pinlau.

I'd never heard of the Pinlau or of any tribe with anything like the Wai.

'He was a young boy when he saw it.'

'How old?'

Nell asked him. He shook his head. She asked again. 'Five or six, he thinks.'

I tried to calculate how long ago that would have been. He was exceptionally old for the region, his face shrunken, his features collapsing to the center, and his left earlobe nearly horizontal on a large growth coming out of the top of his jawbone. Hairless, toothless, a thumb and one finger on each hand, he had to be over ninety. He understood immediately that although Nell was speaking, the questions were mine, and he looked at me directly when answering, his eyes clear, free of the glaucoma which blued the eyes of so many natives, even children.

'It was a ceremony?'

'Yes.'

How often was it practiced?' I asked.

'I saw very little,' Nell translated. She hadn't asked him my question. She had asked him what he'd seen. I smiled at this and she shrugged. She asked again.

He didn't know. Nell reminded him that he couldn't say that. She had put a taboo on that response.

'I remember little.'

'What were these little things you saw?'

'I saw my mother's skirt.'

'Who was wearing your mother's skirt?'

At this Chanta looked ashamed. 'Tell him it is common,' I said. 'Tell him it is very common for the Kiona.'

She did, and Chanta looked back and forth between us with his clear eyes, unsure if we were making a joke. 'Tell him this is true. Tell him I have lived with Kiona for two years.'

Chanta's incredulity only seemed to grow. He seemed to be retreating.

Nell chose her words carefully. She spoke for many sentences, pointing to me as she might a blackboard in a lecture hall. Using a careful grave tone, nearly worshipful.

'I saw my uncle and my father in courting clothes,' he said.

'Can you describe them?'

'Cowrie necklaces, mother-of-pearl collar, waistbands, leaf skirts. The things girls used to wear. In those days.'

'And what were they doing in these clothes, your uncle and father?'

'They were walking around in a circle.'

'And then?'

'They kept walking.'

'And what did the people watching do?'

'They laughed.'

'They thought it was funny?'

'Very funny.'

'And then?'

He started to say something and stopped. We urged him on.

'And then my mother came out of the bushes. And my aunt and my girl cousins.'

'And what were they wearing?'

'Bones through their noses, paint, mud.'

'Where were they painted?'

'Their face and chests and backs.'

'They were dressed as men?'

'Yes.'

'As warriors?'

'Yes.'

'Were they wearing anything else?'

'No.'

'What else did they do?'

'I didn't see the rest.'

'Why not?'

'I left.'

'Why?'

Silence. The water in his eyes trembled. This was clearly an upsetting memory. I thought we should stop.

'What were the women wearing?' Nell asked again.

He didn't answer.

'What were the women wearing?'

'I have already said.'

'Have you?'

Silence.

'Did something upset you then?'

'Penis gourds,' he whispered. 'They were wearing penis

gourds. I ran away. I was a silly boy. I did not understand. I ran away.'

'This is what the Kiona women wear, too,' I told him. 'It can be unsettling.'

'The Kiona?' Chanta looked at me with relief. And then he laughed, a great bark of a laugh.

'What is funny?'

'I was a silly boy.' And then he was overcome with laughter. 'My mother wore a penis gourd,' he squeaked, and his face crumpled even further until he was just a pair of wet eyes and a smooth wedge of black upper gums. He seemed to be emptying his body of a great deal of tension.

Nell was laughing with him and I wasn't sure what had just happened: who had asked the questions, whose questions were asked, how we got that story out of him when he did not want to tell it, when he had kept it as a secret all his life. Bolunta. They *want* to tell their stories, she had said once, they just don't always know how. I'd had years of school, and years in the field, but my real education, this method of persistence I would draw on for the rest of my career, happened right then with Nell.

After lunch she gathered a few things in a bag.

'You're off on your rounds now?'

'I'll keep it short today. I won't go to the other hamlets, just the women's houses here.'

'Don't change your plans for me. I'll go and find Kanup. Follow him around a bit.'

'I'm sorry Fen has done this. Made off with your canoe. Kept you stuck here.'

'I'm not stuck. I could pay someone to get me back if I wanted to go.' I flushed at my honesty.

She smiled. She was beautiful standing there in a ripped shirt over wide cotton trousers, a bilum bag slung over her shoulder. 'Take cigarettes with you,' she said, and left.

Kanup was eager to hear what I knew of Fen and Xambun's hunt. That is what they all thought—that Fen and Xambun had gone on a boar hunt. He led me to a back room of his men's house where, he told me, the men were discussing this expedition. I sat on a thick cane mat and passed out the cigarettes, which quickly made me many pals. Chanta was there and broke into laughter every time our eyes met. Kanup did his best to translate, though it was clearly not a skill of his and I got only fragments of the long conversation. Now that Xambun was gone, they felt free to speak of him. Some of the men felt slighted not to have been included on the trip, but the general feeling was that it was a good thing he had gone. His spirit has gone wandering, they said. He had not returned with it. He was once a man on fire and he came back a man of ash. He is not the same man, they said, and he has gone to find his spirit and bring it back into his body. They appealed to his ancestors, reciting their long names, and to the land and water spirits. I watched how fervently they prayed to all their gods for the return of Xambun's soul to his body. Tears sprung from their clenched eyes and sweat beaded on their arms. I doubted anyone had ever prayed for me like that, or any other way for that matter.

*   *   *

I didn't hear her come up. I was typing up the day's notes.

'I love that sound,' she said just outside the netting, and I jumped.

'I hope you're not bothered. My notes turn to mush quickly if I don't get them down.'

'Mine too.' She was bright and lovely, grinning at me. 'I'm nearly through.'

'Take as long as you like. That's Fen's machine anyway.'

She went to her bedroom and came back with another typewriter. She set it on the adjacent desk. I tried to concentrate, though I was aware of her legs to the left of mine beneath the table and her fingers feeding a page into the platen and her lips fluttering slightly as she read over her notes. Once she began typing, at a furious rate that was not at all surprising, the sound concentrated my thoughts and our keys thundered together. I noticed that she was manually advancing the paper at the end of each line. It was a lovely instrument, dove grey with ivory keys, but it was dented in one corner and the silver arm had broken off at its base.

She ripped out a page and snapped in another.

'I don't believe you're writing actual words,' I said.

She handed me her first page. There were no paragraphs, barely any punctuation, the thinnest sliver of a margin. *Tavi sits still her eyes drooping nearly asleep body swaying and Mudama carefully pinching the lice flicking the bugs in the fire the zinging of her fingernails through the strands of hair, concentration tenderness love peace pieta.*

I looked down at my own words: *In light of this conversation with Chanta, and the proximity of his native Pinlau to the Kiona, one concludes that there were other tribes in the vicinity who also once practiced some sort of transvestite ritual.*

'You're writing some sort of avant-garde novel,' I said.

'I just want to be able to put myself back in that moment when I read it over a year from now. What I think is important now might not be important to me then. If I can remember the *feeling* of sitting next to Mudama and Tavi on this afternoon then I can recall all the details I didn't think important enough to write down.'

I tried it her way. I wrote a full description of Chanta and his tumor and his hands without fingers and his wet clear eyes. I wrote down all the dialogue I could remember, which was much more than I had in my notes, though at the time I thought I was getting everything down. I loved the sound of our two typewriters; it felt like we were in a band, making a strange sort of music. It felt like I was a part of something, and that the work was important. She always made me feel that the work was important. And then her typewriter stopped and she was watching me. 'Don't stop,' I said. 'Your typing makes my brain work better.'

When we finished we ate dried fish and old sago pancakes. Through the doorway there were long flashes of lightning. There was a rumbling that I thought was thunder.

She lit a mosquito coil and we sat in the doorway with mugs of tea.

'Drums,' she said. 'Fen and Xambun's beats. They are wishing them safety at night.'

I told her about the talk in the men's house and their hope that Xambun's spirit would return to him. We could hear people gathering near the drums. A few women passed below the house, their children lagging behind, one with a knitted doll Nell must have given her. Lightning was still flashing, silently, behind the northern hills where the moon would soon rise. I felt the world had finally carved out a little place for me.

We talked of our Grid.

'Personality depends on context, just like culture,' she said. 'Certain people bring out certain traits in each other. Don't you think? If I had a husband, for example, who said, "Your typing makes my brain work better," I would not be so ashamed of my impulse to work. You don't always see how much other people are shaping you. What are you looking at?'

I wasn't looking at much of anything. I was just trying not to look at her. No sign of the moon, and the lake wasn't visible save in the few seconds that the lightning flashed. But the air was shifting. I felt something that was almost a cool wind against my arms and face, but not a wind, not even a breeze, just an air current that felt different, as if someone ten feet away had opened the lid of an ice box briefly. I reached out to feel it and, as if I had beckoned it, a great gust struck against my hand. All at once the trees shuddered and the grass skirt about the house swished.

'Let's go down to the sand and make the rain come,' she said.

'What?'

'Let's do a dance, like the Zuni.'

And then she was down the ladder, racing to the path. I followed. Of course I followed.

Neither of us knew an actual rain dance, but we improvised. She claimed ami was the Zuni word for rain. It was cheating because the rain was coming, everything was shifting so fast, the wind had worked the tall palms into a froth above us and scudded hard against the water and the sky was low and black. But we stomped on the sand and called out Ami! Ami! and every other word we knew for rain and wet and water, and everything suddenly got blacker and cooler and the wind fierce and the memory of rain, real rain, came on quickly, only a few moments before the rain itself. We held our faces up and spread out our arms. Big drops smacked all over us and drove the insects on our skin to the ground.

The rain hit the lake water loudly and it took my ears several minutes to get used to the roar. You don't realize in the dry season how much is held in, but now all the sounds and smells came back, stirred up by the wind and humidity, flowers and roots and leaves exhaling their full flavor. Even the lake itself released a pungent peat odor as the rain dug into it. Nell seemed smaller and younger and I could see her easily at thirteen, at nine, a little girl on a Pennsylvania farm, and all I could do was keep looking. I hardly knew I wasn't speaking. 'I think we should go in,' she said.

I thought she meant go back to the house, but she turned from me and unbuttoned her dress and dropped it in the sand. She walked to the water in a brassiere and short American knickers, loose at the thigh. 'I can't swim, so you better join me.'

I quickly pulled off my shirt and trousers. The water was warmer than the air and felt like the first bath I'd had in two years. I sank in up to my neck and let my feet float to the surface as the rain hammered the water as if it were a sheet of silver.

She really couldn't swim. How had I not noticed this before? I paddled around but she remained upright, bouncing on her toes. Of course I wanted to offer to teach her, to hold her as my mother had held me in the River Cam, to feel the weight of her in my arms, the edge of her brassiere against my fingers, knickers thin and wet as they broke the surface. I could feel it far too well without actually doing it, and I found I had to keep swimming away from her to try and subdue the effects, then swimming back to hear what she was saying through the smashing rain.

The rain was still lashing as we ran back up to the house. We put on dry clothes, each in the dark of our respective mosquito rooms. I fished out some old-looking Australian biscuits from the hoard and she asked if I was never not hungry. I said I was twice her size which led to an argument about how many inches were between us which led to measuring each other against a post, marking the spot with a penknife then calculating the difference. I held the measuring tape out flat, my fingers damp from the swim and dusty from all the biscuits. Seventeen inches.

'It seems like more when it's horizontal like that. Up and down it doesn't seem so dramatic, does it?'

We were standing close by the pole and she was cheating by standing on her toes, her face lifted straight up and the rain crashing into the thatch above us and I wasn't sure how I would kiss her without lifting her up to my lips. She laughed as if I had said this out loud.

We went back to the sofa and somehow I told her about Aunt Dottie and the New Forest and my trip to the Galápagos in '22. 'My father had hoped the trip would make a biologist out of me but the only valuable thing I discovered was that my body loves a hot, humid climate. Unlike yours.' I nearly brushed my fingers along her scarred arm beside mine.

'I come from hearty Pennsylvania potato farmers on my mother's side. You'll have to see me in winter. The cold gives me energy.'

I laughed. 'I'm not sure I want to see what that looks like.' But I did. More than anything I could think of.

She told me more about her potato-growing ancestors and their escape from the Great Famine, which put me in mind of Yeats's 'The Ballad of Father Gilligan,' and we ended up saying poems back and forth.

After the war I'd memorized most of Brooke and Owen and Sassoon, and half convinced myself that they'd been written by John. Or Martin, who actually did write poetry. The war poets were all tangled up with my brothers and my youth and I thought I would cry when I got to the end of 'Hardness of Heart' and the bit about tears not being endless, but I didn't. Nell did the crying for both of us.

I try not to return to these moments very often, for I end up lacerating my young self for not simply kissing the girl. I thought we had time. Despite everything, I believed somehow there was time. Love's first mistake. Perhaps love's only mistake. Time for you and time for me, though I never did warm to Eliot. She was married. She was pregnant. And what would it have mattered in the end? What would it have altered to have kissed her then, that night? Everything. Nothing. Impossible to know.

We fell asleep reciting. Who was speaking or what poem I am not certain. We woke to little Sema and Amini poking us in the leg.

25

The morning began as the one before, with children scrambling in and out of her lap, and hand games and explosions of laughter. Bani brought me coffee and I worked at her typewriter. A few boys peered in through the netting. Chanta didn't come but I thought more about my conversation with him and jotted down some questions for Teket when I returned.

All at once, far too early, Nell scooted everyone out of the house.

'What's going on?' I called to her.

'No mothers,' she said. 'No adult women today.' She began packing her visiting bag. She was wearing the blue dress I'd first seen her in. 'Something is going on. It happened last month and they wouldn't let me in. I'm not going to be brushed off this time. I'll be back at teatime.' And she was gone.

By teatime Fen might be back, too.

I spent a few hours at their bookshelves and the piles of books around them. They had brought so many books, American novels I'd never heard of, ethnographies that had won prizes I didn't know about, books by sociologists and psychologists with strange names from places like California and Texas.

It was a whole universe I barely knew existed. They had a mound of magazines, too. I read about Roosevelt's election and something called the Cyclotron, an atom-smasher that forced particles around in circles to accelerations of over a million electron volts, at which point they broke and formed a new kind of radium. I would have stayed in reading all day, but Kanup came round to ask if I wanted to go fishing.

I followed him down to the water. The sky was clear and the sun beat down, but the ground was pocked and shredded from the storm, littered with huge fronds and leaves, nuts and hard unripe fruits. We crunched through piles of debris to get to his boat on the beach. Many canoes were already on the water, paddled by men. I asked him why the men were fishing today, and not the women.

He smiled and said the women were busy. He seemed to want to imply more, but not say it. 'The women are crazy today,' he said.

We checked our nets and headed out. The Tam men were born and bred to be artisans: potters, painters, and mask makers. They were, I learned that afternoon, staggeringly poor fishermen. They argued and insulted one another. Their fingers ripped holes in the fragile fiber nets. They didn't seem to understand how the traps worked. Their loud voices scared the fish. I had a good chuckle watching them, but all the while I was aware of the far side of the lake, dimly shimmering, from where at any moment my canoe would reappear.

I was glad when we got back to shore, eager for tea with Nell and what little time alone with her remained. But Kanup wanted to wash out the canoe, which he thought smelled of fish though he hadn't caught anything, and plug up a small leak, so we went to get some gum sap from his house. I called up to Nell as we went by, but there was no answer.

When we returned to the beach she was standing ankle-deep in the water, both hands shielding her eyes, scouring the surface of the lake. Kanup was talking and she turned about and saw us. Her arms dropped to her sides.

'They told me you'd left!'

'Left?'

'Yes. Chanta told me you'd gone off in a boat.'

'I went fishing with Kanup.'

'Oh, thank God.' She grabbed me by my shirtsleeves. 'I really thought you'd gone to find them.'

'Bit late for that.'

Kanup had gone over to his canoe, but I did not follow to help him because Nell hadn't let me go. She held on and examined the fabric of my plain white shirt. There was something different about her.

'I thought you'd gone to Bett,' she said.

'Bett?'

'Because she has a boat.'

I'd forgotten about Bett and her boat. And that I'd told Fen about her.

'I'm sorry,' she said laughing, though she seemed to be crying, too. She let go of my shirtsleeves and brushed at her face quickly. 'I've had a very strange day, Bankson.'

I could not take my eyes off her. It was as if she were performing some trick, some sort of unfolding. There was something raw and exposed about her, as if many things had already happened between us, as if time had leapt ahead and we were already lovers. 'What's happened?'

'Let's go up to the house.'

I gave Kanup an apologetic shrug, which I wasn't sure he understood. But nothing could have separated me from Nell at that moment. I took one last fearful glance at the horizon. Empty. A bit more time. I followed her closely up the path.

We didn't have tea. She poured us whiskey, and we sat across from each other at the kitchen table. 'I don't know if you'll believe me.'

'Of course I will.'

She stood up. 'Sorry, I think I should write it all up first.' She went to her desk and slid a piece of paper into her type-writer. I waited for the rush of keys. Nothing. She came back and sat down at the table. 'I think maybe I do need to tell you.' She took a long sip of her whiskey. She had a lovely throat, unmarred by the tropics. When she put the glass down she looked at me directly.

'If I tried to tell Fen this, he wouldn't believe me. He'd say I'd made it up, or mis—'

'Tell me, Nell.'

'As soon as I turned up the women's road, I felt it, the same queer stillness as that one other time when they kept me out. I went straight to the last house, where smoke was coming out of all three chimneys and all the windows were sealed tight. I pushed through the curtain before anyone could stop me and was struck in the face by hot stinky wet air, like a smelly steam house. I gagged and tried to stick my nose out the doorway for some air but Malun pulled me in and took my basket and told me it was the *minyana* and they'd all decided I could stay.'

The *minyana*. She hadn't heard this word before, she told me. When her eyes adapted to the dark room, she made out round black slabs of something cooking in small amounts of water on pans in the hearths. The room was full of women, many more than usual, and no one was mending a line or weaving a basket or nursing a baby. There were no children at all. Some of the women tended the pans on the fire and others were lying on mats along all sides of the room. All at once the black slabs were flipped over. They made a great clatter. They were stones, smooth round stones cooking in flat earthen pans. The women then left the stones and came away from the fire, carrying small pots they had been warming. Each woman on a mat was paired with a woman at the fire. An old woman named Yepe led Nell to a mat. 'I tried to get my notebook from my basket but she stopped me and made me lie down.' Yepe squatted next to her and unfastened her dress clumsily, inexperienced with buttons. Then she dipped her hands into the pot. They came out thick and dripping with oil and she placed them on Nell's neck and began a slow massage, working her way down her back slowly, kneading, her hands moving easily in the thick oil. 'It was happening like this all down the rows of mats, the massages deepening, quickening, and the women—you have to understand, these women are hardworking and unpampered; the Tam men are the ones who have much more leisure, who sit around painting their pots and their bodies and gossiping—these women started grunting and groaning.'

Nell got up for the whiskey bottle, and when she came back she took the seat sideways to mine, filled our glasses, and put her feet on the rungs of my chair. 'You're sure you want me to go on?'

'Quite sure.'

The massage became erotic. Yepe's hands slid under her and cupped her breasts and rubbed her nipples with her thumb and moved to the buttocks and pushed the flesh hard up and down and pressed her fingers against the anus. The women on the mats were making a good deal of noise now, their bodies no longer passive but pushing up against the hands. Some of the women on the mats tried to reach between their legs or turn over but they were not allowed. Bo nun, someone said. Not yet. Yepe returned to her hearth and with a forked stick lifted steaming stones from the pans and placed them on a strip of bark cloth and brought them back. The women on the mats flipped over all at once. They cried out as the stones were rubbed with oil.

'Well, you can probably imagine the rest,' she said.

'No, I can't. I have an awful imagination.'

'Yepe placed a stone here.' She undid a few of the white front buttons of her blue dress and put my hand flat on her stomach. 'And moved it in slow circles.' Her skin was still oiled, still warm. I kept my circles small and slow on her taut belly, though I wanted to touch every bone, every patch of her. I wanted every part of her pressed against me.

'Slowly, she pushed it up, up and along the collarbone.' I did what she said and my hand, passing through, grazed her breasts (no brassiere today), which were fuller than I'd guessed, and traveled the ridge of her collarbone several times. 'And down again, back and forth across the nipples.' She watched me. I watched her. Our eyes had not lowered or shut.

So often a woman's pleasure felt to me a mystery, the slightest wisp of a thing you were meant to find, and she having no better idea of where to look than you did.

'Then she turned the stone on its side and brought it down—'

I kissed her. Or, as Nell later claimed, I leapt at her. I could not touch enough of her at once. I don't remember removing clothes, hers or mine, but we were naked and laughing at our groping and when she reached down and felt me she smiled and said it wasn't quite a stone, but it would do.

'Well, that's a relief,' she said as we lay stuck together, mottled in bugs and dirt.

'Is it?'

'Remember elephants in large boots?'

'The ink blot?'

'That was the sex card. You're supposed to see something sexual. And you said elephants in large boots. It had me worried. Listen to that.'

Sounds came from every direction—the beach, the gardens, the fields behind the women's road.

If I hadn't understood, I might not have said it was human.

'Lots of sex tonight,' she said. 'The men are a bit threatened by the stones, apparently. The night of the minyana they need to be reassured that their women still want them.'

'Reassure away.'

* * *

We did not sleep that night. We moved to my mat and talked and pressed our bodies together. She told me the Tam believed that love grows in the stomach and that they went around clutching their bellies when their hearts were broken. 'You are in my stomach' was their most intimate expression of love.

We knew that Fen could return at any moment, but we did not mention it.

'The Mumbanyo kill their twins,' she told me close to morning, 'because two babies meant two different lovers.' It was the only time she alluded to him or her pregnancy.

We did not hear Bani come up. He must have been standing there awhile, trying at first to give our spirits time to return to our bodies, for when he did rouse us his voice was loud and fed up. 'Nell-Nell!' His lips were touching the thin ghostly netting. 'Fen di lam,' he said. 'Mirba tun.'

She leapt up as if a snake had bitten her. Bani went back down the ladder. 'He's halfway across the lake.'

'Bugger.'

'Yes, bugga,' she mimicked. I touched her back as she groped around for her dress, and she stopped and kissed me, and I felt, stupidly, that it would all be okay.

We needn't have hurried. When we reached the shore the boat was still far off. We could have stayed in bed, made love one more time.

'He's cut the engine too soon.' I knew I'd now find any fault with him I could. 'It wouldn't disturb anyone from all the way out there.' He'd tried to sneak up on us, I suspected.

Nell was shielding her eyes with her hand, though it was not a bright morning. There seemed to be no sun at all in the low metal-colored sky. It wasn't raining, but it felt like we were breathing water. I wanted her to reach for me, claim me, but she stood rigid as a meerkat, focused on the boat, still a blemish, coming slowly toward shore. I touched the back of her neck, the short hairs that had come loose from her plait. I felt as wide open and undefended as a man can be.

'Please dear God don't let him have that flute,' Nell said.

The outlines of the figures in the boat sharpened: one seated in the stern, one standing amidships. But they were still so far away. I wanted to go back to bed with her and resented this standing and waiting I had to do before he took her back. And I resented Bani for stealing these last minutes from me, even though Fen might have found her lying in my arms.

Bani and a few other boys were farther down the beach, talking boisterously and laughing, reliving, I was sure, the night before, rehearsing their stories for Xambun.

Nell was squinting. She'd left her glasses behind. 'What do you see?' she asked. 'They're saying it was a good hunt. They're saying they've got something big, a boar or a buck.'

For a few moments that's what it looked like: a good hunt, an animal slumped over the bow of my thin canoe.

And then one of Bani's friends let out a scream. And I saw what he saw.

The standing figure in the middle was not a man but a long thick pole, the paddling figure in the stern was Fen, and what had looked like an animal carcass was Xambun draped diagonally in the bow.

'What is it, Andrew?' Nell wailed. I think it was the only time she ever said my first name.

I wrapped her in my arms and told her quietly in her ear. Behind us the screaming began and never stopped. The sides of my canoe were streaked with blood. When the boat came close enough, Bani and the other boys waded out up to their necks to reach Xambun. They lifted his body up off the boat and carried it high in their arms toward land.

Fen was saying the same thing over and over: Fua nengaina fil. I didn't know what it meant. There was splashing and wailing and Xambun was handed over to Malun, who had come running and shrieking onto the beach. She sank to the wet sand with her son, his blood no longer running and his skin the color of driftwood. Nell pulled away from me and went to her. She wrapped her arms around Malun, but Malun threw her off. She hollered and shook Xambun, tears, spit, and sweat coming off her as she moved, as if she believed that with enough force she could bend back the universe.

Fen squatted in the shallows beside Nell. His face was narrower than I remembered, a blade slicing the air, his forehead white but the rest stained with blood. His shirtfront was caked with it as well.

'Fua nengaina fil,' he cried out to them, as if he were still in the boat and they were hundreds of yards away. He spoke directly to Malun and tears cut pale lines through the dried blood on his face. Malun, when she registered him, screeched like an animal that had been bitten. With her two arms she shoved him away from her son's body.

'It wasn't my fault, Nell. They ambushed us. Kolekamban ambushed us.'

I could see the arrow wounds: one in the temple, one in the chest. Clean, precise shots.

More and more people were coming onto the beach, encircling us, pressing in to see Xambun. I could barely breathe. From somewhere behind us a slit drum started up, awful, powerful, drawn-out knells loud enough for every person and spirit on the lake to hear. The sound shook through me.

I crouched next to Fen. 'Did they see it was you?' I said.

He lifted his mess of a face to me and seemed to break into a smile. 'No! No one saw me. I was invisible.' He turned to Nell. 'I used the spell and I was invisible.'

But Nell was still trying to hold Malun, trying to reach her and comfort her in her hysteria.

'Did they see you leave with the flute?' I asked Fen.

'They couldn't see me. Only Xambun.'

'If they saw you, they'll come after you.'

'They didn't see me, Bankson. Nellie.' He grabbed Nell's face and turned it to his. 'Nellie, I'm sorry.' His head lurched and fell against her chest and he heaved up sobs that no one could hear in the chaos.

I broke out of the circle and fetched my boat, which had drifted downshore. I pulled it back toward the path that led to their house. The flute was wrapped in towels and tied up with the twine from Helen's manuscript. It was as thick as a man's thigh. I took it out then flipped the boat. Blood and water funneled out into the sand. I set it to rights, and as I straightened up I felt light-headed and sat down. All around me people had given over to grief, weeping and keening and singing in groups in the sand, the women's skin still glistening with oil from the day before.

Several men I didn't recognize, older men who had already covered themselves with funereal mud, approached the canoe. One examined the engine without touching it, keeping his distance in case it roared to life, but the other two went straight for the flute and began plucking at the twine.

Fen called out something and came running.

'Jesus, Bankson, don't let them touch it.' He reached out for the tall bundle but the two men pulled it away. Fen lunged for it, seized it with one arm and shoved off the men with the other.

'Be careful, Fen. Be very careful right now,' I said quietly.

The largest man began asking questions, one after the other, urgent but precise. Fen answered solemnly. At one point he broke down, and seemed to be offering a long apology. The large man had no patience for this. He held up his hand then pointed to the flute. Fen told him no. He asked again and Fen said no more sharply, which put an end to the conversation.

After they walked away Fen said, 'They want to bury the flute with Xambun.'

'Seems the least you could do for them, given—'

'Stick it in the ground to rot? After everything I went through?'

'Now is not the time to upset them.'

'Oh, is now not the time?' he mimicked bitterly. 'Are you an expert on my tribe, too?'

'A man has been murdered, Fen.'

'Just stay out of it, Bankson, all right? Will you do that for once?' He lifted the flute and carried it awkwardly away.

The three men had moved down the beach to where a larger group of men gathered around the slit drum. But the drumming had stopped as the players listened to what the mud-painted men had to say.

I knew what was happening. They were all realizing that it had not been a hunt but a raid Fen had taken Xambun on, and that now Fen was unwilling to share the spoils with Xambun's spirit. Without the flute, Xambun would be restless, would make trouble for them all. They had to get it. I could see it in their eyes. It was perhaps just the beginning of what they would need to avenge Xambun's death.

I pushed my way back in to Nell.

Her eyes were shut. Malun was calmer and letting Nell stroke her back.

'We need to go. We need to leave here now.' I pressed my cheek to her temple, her hair against my lips. 'We do. We need to go.'

Without opening her eyes, she said, 'We can't. Not now. Not like this.'

'Listen to me.' I took both her arms. 'We need to get in my boat and go.'

She yanked herself out of my grip. 'I'm not going anywhere. I'm not leaving her.'

'It's not safe, Nell. No one is safe.'

'I know them. They won't hurt us. They're not like your Kiona.'

'They want the flute.'

'Let them have the flute.'

'He'll never give it to them, Nell. He'll die before he does.'

'We can't go. These are my people.' Her voice broke. She understood. She understood about their gods and amends— and Fen's brutal possessiveness.

Her small face was smeared with blood and sand and she looked as if she'd never resented someone more than she resented me and my good sense. She resisted a little while longer then I guided her out and up the beach.

People were still streaming onto the sand from the road. I saw Chanta and Kanup and little Luquo, who was screaming for his brother. But no one stopped us. The men by the drums watched us move away but they did not come after us.

Fen was in a chair, the flute leaning up beside him. Nell went straight to her bedroom. He jumped up and followed her.

'Don't come in here.'

'Nell, I need to tell you something.'

'No.'

'I talked to Abapenamo. They did give it to me. The flute was a gift. It's rightfully mine.'

'You think I care who owns it now? You got a man killed for it, Fen. Xambun is *dead*.'

'I know, Nellie. I know.' He slid to the ground and wrapped his arms around her legs.

A raw loathing coursed through me. 'Get up, Fen,' I said through the netting. 'Pack your bags. We're leaving.'

I got the canoe and brought it around to a smaller beach where they met me. We loaded it up with my suitcases, their duffels, and the small trunk. I'd found her specs by my mat and handed them to her when Fen wasn't looking. She put them on without acknowledgment of anything else and turned back to the other beach, the entire village gathered there now.

'Don't call attention to anything,' I said quietly. 'Just get in the boat.'

Fen and his flute got in. 'It's out of petrol, you know,' he said, as if that were my fault. 'I had to paddle most of the way back.'

Good, I thought. Gave me more time with your wife.

'I've another jug right here,' I said. 'You left it when you stole my boat.'

I affixed the petrol line to the new jug and gave it a pump. The motor turned over on the first try. A few small heads lifted and turned. Only the children playing in the water heard the sound of the engine.

'Baya ban!' little Amini hollered from the shallows.

Nell raised herself up and in a low cracked voice called out, 'Baya ban!'

'Baya ban!'

'Baya ban!' Nell called. I wanted to tell her to stop, but the men by the drums on the far side of the beach seemed not to hear her in the tumult.

Nell warbled out every long name of each child waving to her, complete with clan and maternal and paternal ancestor names, until her words gave out and her wailing became incoherent. The children waded deeper into the water as we pulled away and splashed madly at our boat, screaming out things I couldn't understand.

Go. Go to your beautiful dances, your beautiful ceremonies. And we will bury our dead.

The sky seemed so low, so bleak. For a moment I lost my bearings entirely, and I wasn't even sure where to point the boat, how to get back to the river. Then I remembered the canal between the hills and I pushed up the throttle and the motor drowned out all their voices. The canoe lifted, lurched, then skimmed fast across the black lake.

We flagged down a pinnace almost as soon as we reached the Sepik proper. It was a boat full of missionaries from Glasgow who planned to sprinkle themselves and their faith all over the region. I could see their hearty confidence falter as soon as they saw us.

'Been through the wars, have ye?' one of them managed, but they shrunk from us as soon as we climbed on board. Nor did we give them much opportunity for conversation, though one of them bought my canoe and engine for far more than they were worth. Nell tried to persuade me not to sell, to go directly back to the Kiona. But I was determined to go with them to Sydney, and I needed the money. While Fen was up talking to the driver about getting the rest of their stuff picked up, I told her I'd go as far as New York with her if she'd let me. She shut her eyes and Fen came back to his seat beside her before she had answered.

26

We took rooms in Sydney at the Black Opal in George Street. Nell insisted on having her own. The clerk wrote down in his ledger Nell Stone, Andrew Bankson, Schuyler Fenwick, and it pleased me to see their names separated and to see Nell receive her own key, 319, a flight above the rooms Fen and I were given.

Without bathing, we walked to the Commonwealth Bank then down to the White Star booking office where Nell and Fen secured two passages to New York. I'd hoped they'd have to wait weeks for space on a ship, but because of the crook economy, the man in the office said, most liners were half empty. The SS *Calgaric* would sail in four days. The paper money they slid across the counter looked fake. An electric fan spun bland air at us, though the day was cool and Nell wore a sweater over her blouse that made her look like a girl at university. Everything felt wrong: the fan, the hard floor, the man's combed hair and bow tie, the smells of cured leather and mint candy. I wanted my own ticket on that liner. I wanted to tear up hers and take her back to the Kiona with me.

Unable to return to the heavy walls of the Black Opal, unable to sit at a restaurant, we walked. I tried to inure myself to the noise, the foot and road traffic, the hundreds of bloated pink faces barking in Australian English, which had become a loathsome sound. Even the shop signs and billboards over-whelmed me. YOUR GAS REFRIGERATOR, MADAM, IS HERE. THE BEST THINGS IN LIFE COME IN CELLOPHANE. Nevertheless, I was compelled to read every one.

This sensation of the familiar feeling new and jarring was something I had relished when I'd returned from my first field trip. This time it felt wretched. I had never seen more clearly how streets like these were made for and by amoral cowards, men who made money in rubber or sugar or copper or steel in remote places then returned here where no one questioned their practices, their treatment of others, their greed. Like them, the three of us would face no recrimina-tions. No one would ever ask us here how we had got a man killed.

Before Fen had seen the numbers, I had chosen Room 219, the one directly below Nell's. Next morning, when I heard her door open and shut, I dressed quickly and went down to the breakfast room. They hadn't started serving yet and the room was empty save Nell in the corner holding a teacup with two hands as if it were a coconut gourd. I took the seat across from her. Neither of us had slept.

'The only thing worse than being out of that room is being in that room,' she said.

I wanted to say so much. I wanted to acknowledge with her what had happened, how we had let it happen, why we had let it happen. I wanted to tell her Fen had made it clear to me from the start that this flute was what he was after and that I had done nothing to stop him, only taken full advantage of his absence. But I wanted to say it all lying down again with her, holding her in my arms. 'I should have gone after him straightaway, as soon as I saw the note.'

'You couldn't have caught up with him.' She ran her finger along the edge of the teacup. 'And you certainly wouldn't have persuaded him otherwise.' She was wearing the sweater again. She hadn't looked up at me yet.

'I wanted that time with you,' I said. 'I wanted it more than I've wanted anything in my life.' These last words surprised me. The truth of them made me start to shake. When she didn't respond, I said, 'I can't regret that. It was perfect.'

'Worth a man's life?'

'Was what worth a man's life?' Fen said. He'd come in a side door behind me.

'Your flute,' Nell said.

He frowned, as if she were a child who'd been cheeky, and told an approaching waiter to fetch him a chair. He'd bathed and shaved and smelled like the West.

Again we wandered. We walked through the Art Gallery of New South Wales. We looked at the watercolors by Julian Ashton and a new exhibit of Aboriginal bark paintings. We sat at a café with tables outdoors, like in the *New Yorker* drawing. We ordered things we hadn't seen in years: veal, Welsh rarebit, spaghetti. But none of us ate more than a few bites of any of it.

On the way back to the Black Opal I saw that Nell's limp was worse.

'It's not my ankle,' she said. 'It's these shoes I haven't worn for two years.'

When we passed a chemist's I stayed back and slipped inside. The girl behind the counter looked part Aboriginal, rare for a shopkeeper in Sydney then. She passed me the box without speaking.

'I think I can pay for my wife's plasters,' Fen said, pushing me aside to give her the money.

At the hotel the clerk handed us a note from Claire Iynes, an anthropologist at the University of Sydney, inviting us to dinner.

'How'd she know we were here?' Nell said.

'I rang her up yesterday,' Fen said.

He wanted to tell her about the flute.

'Dinner? How are we to go to a dinner, Fen?'

'There's a dress shop two doors down, miss,' the clerk said. 'Hair and beauty across the street. Fix you up smart.'

A cab took us up to Double Bay, where Claire and her husband lived, just above Redleaf Pool.

'Poshy posh,' Fen said out the window to the large houses on the water. He brought his head back in. 'Claire has moved up in the world. What did she marry into?'

'Mining, I think. Silver or copper,' Nell said, the first sentences she'd uttered since we'd gotten the invitation.

Fen smirked at me. 'Bankson doesn't like it when the colonists talk about where money comes from.'

It wasn't a large dinner, nine of us around a small table in what seemed to be a drawing room. The vast dining room was on the other side of the house, too big, we were told, for four couples and the English hanger-on. No one knew quite what to make of my presence. I wasn't headed home; I wasn't finished with my fieldwork. We hadn't thought this through. It highlighted even for us the fact that I'd followed them all the way here with no good reason. I think I had been waiting all along for Fen to say 'Why *are* you here, Bankson? Why don't you leave us the hell alone?' Because my only reason, the reason he knew as well as I, was that I was in love with his wife. He could have called me out anytime, and he could have done it right there with witnesses in the Iyneses' house, but instead he said, 'He's been ill. Seizures. We thought he should see a doctor.'

There was a long discussion about doctors in Sydney and who would be the best for mysterious tropical diseases. Eventually Fen rerouted them with talk of our 'breakthrough,' he called it, our grid, and we spent most of the evening mapping out the guests and mutual acquaintances, of which there were many. One man with a great heavy moustache knew Bett from a project he'd done in Rabaul; another had read zoology with my father at Cambridge. Claire seemed to know every anthropologist we could name, and caught us up on the department gossip in three different countries.

Fen flourished in fresh company, bringing out all the Mumbanyo stories with which he once entertained me. I watched him twirl his wineglass, eat prawns with a sterling silver oyster fork, accept a light from an engraved lighter—this man I'd seen shit off the side of a bark canoe, covered in another man's blood. I saw then that any remorse he'd shown us had been an act. He was exuberant, a man who was just about to seize hold of the best stretch of his life. He fed off of Nell's and my disorientation.

I'd been put beside Mrs. Isabel Swale. Her husband, Arthur, already sozzled when we'd arrived, had drunk himself into an aphasic stupor and followed the conversation stupidly, as a dog follows the ball during a game of tennis. Mrs. Swale badgered me with questions about the Kiona without listening to the answers, so that her inquiry was disjointed and did not create anything resembling a conversation. Her left leg, bare through a slit in her gown, came closer and closer to me and by dessert was pressed alongside my own. All of her gestures—the way she leaned her lips to my ear, knocked her head back in a sudden and inexplicable laugh, examined the black beneath my fingernails—would have indicated to others at the table that we had struck a sudden, intimate connection. Nell shot me a few direct and withering looks, and I found I was pleased to see any emotion for me at all cross her face. At the far end of the table, Fen talked quietly to Claire Iynes.

After dinner, Colonel Iynes invited the men to have a look at his collection of antique weapons, and Claire led the women off through the house for *digestifs* on the back patio. I lagged behind the men, heard Fen drop his voice and tell the Colonel he was in possession of a rare artifact himself, then I turned around. In a narrow passageway before the kitchen, I took Nell's wrist and held her back.

'You do quite well in civilization, particularly with the ladies,' she said. 'Much better than you have let on.'

'Please, let's not play at anything.'

Her face was as pale and hollowed out as when I first met her.

234

'Stay with me,' I said. 'Stay with me and come back to the Kiona. Stay with me and come to England. Stay with me and we'll go anywhere you like. Fiji,' I said desperately. 'Bali.'

'I keep thinking of how when we first arrived we thought Xambun was a god, a spirit. Some powerful dead man. And now he is.' She started to say something else but it got caught and she leaned against me.

I held her as she wept. I stroked her hair, loose and slightly matted. 'Stay here with me. Or let me come with you.'

She pulled me down to kiss her. Warm. Briny.

'I love you,' she said, her lips still against mine. But it meant no.

She was silent on the way back down to the city, and went directly to her room without a word to either of us.

Fen held up a bottle of cognac the Colonel had given him. 'Quick drink? Help us sleep.'

I doubted he had trouble sleeping, but I followed him to his room. I didn't want to go, but there was some part of me that felt we could work this out. In this situation a Kiona man would offer the other fellow a few spears, an axe, and some betel nut, and then the wife was his.

Fen's room was identical to mine but at the other end of the hallway. Same green walls and knitted white counterpane on the single bed. He poured the brandy into two glasses on a tray by the bed and handed me one.

His bags were splayed open by the window but the flute was not among them. There were no closets or wardrobes and it wouldn't have fit in the small chest of drawers by the door.

'It's under the bed.' He set his glass back on the tray and rolled the flute out a few feet. It was still wrapped in towels and tied with twine, but loosely now, as if he'd gotten tired of all the wrapping and unwrapping.

'It's magnificent, Bankson. Better than I remembered. Glyphs carved all over it.' He bent down to untie the string.

'No. Don't. I don't want to see it.'

'Yes, you do.'

He was right. I did. I wanted to prove him a liar. The isolated, alienating Mumbanyo with a logographic system of writing? No. Much as I wanted to prove him wrong, I would not give him the pleasure of unveiling it to me. 'I don't, Fen.'

'Suit yourself. You'll have to wait until it's under glass then. Claire and the Colonel think I'll have my pick of museums, when I'm ready.' He sat on the bed and pointed to a black chair against the wall. 'Pull up a seat.'

The swaddled flute lay on the floor between us. I drank my cognac fast, in two sips. I planned to stand up and leave, but Fen refilled my glass before I had moved.

'I did not steal it,' he said. 'It was given to me in a ceremony two nights before we left. They taught me how to care for it and feed it and it was when I was spooning a bit of dried fish to its mouth that I saw the writing etched into the wood. Abapenamo said only great men could be taught it. I asked if I was a great man and he said I was. Then Kolekamban busted in with his three brothers. He said the flute had always belonged to their clan, not Abapenamo's, and they grabbed it. A few of Abapenamo's men wanted to go after him but I knew it would end badly. So I stopped them. I kept the peace. Abapenamo's son told me where they would take it and I figured I could come back. I knew I couldn't leave the region without it. You can't walk away from a piece of the human puzzle. But I wanted to get it back peaceably, without anyone getting hurt.'

I let the miserable failure of that plan hang in the room. I thought of how initially he'd asked me to be his partner on this mission, asked me to risk my life for his delusions. I could have been the corpse in the canoe.

'Why didn't they shoot at you, Fen?'

'I told you. I used the Dobu spell.'

'Fen.'

I could tell he wanted to convince me of this, but he also wanted to keep my attention. He was like a little boy who didn't want to be left alone in the dark. 'I think Xambun wanted to die,' he said. 'I think he tried to die.'

'What?' I said.

'The first night we slept a few hours in the bush outside the village. I woke up and found him holding my revolver.'

'Pointing it at something?'

'No, just holding it in his hands. I don't think he wanted to kill me. He might have been working up the courage to shoot *himself*. I took it away and he never reached for it again. We sorted out our route and waited till sunset. He was stealthy and quiet, probably an excellent hunter, but once we got the flute he got careless, like he wanted someone to know we were there. We were far away from the village but some dogs heard us first. I knew we could still make it to the canoe and we did, but he wouldn't lie down. He started screaming a bunch of nonsense and I would have shoved him down but I had to start the engine and steer us out of there. I don't get it. I promised him a quarter of the cash from this thing.'

It was hard to know how much to believe. I wasn't sure it mattered anyway. Xambun was dead. The S S *Calgaric* would leave the next day at noon.

I made to get up from my black chair.

'I saw you on the beach with her,' he said. 'I knew what would happen. I'm not stupid. You knew I'd go and I knew you wouldn't stop me. But you can't have Nell like you can have other girls. She says she's Southern but she's not on the Grid. She's a different type altogether. Trust me on that one.'

He refilled my glass. We'd nearly drunk the bottle.

'What type is she?'

'Damned if I ever let you find out.'

This time I did get up. He stood, too.

'I had to get that flute,' he said. 'Don't you understand? There has to be a balance. A man can't be without power—it doesn't work like that. What was I going to do, write little books behind hers like a fucking echo? I needed something big. And this is big. Books on this thing will write themselves.'

'In blood-red ink, Fen.'

On the way back down the hallway were the stairs to the third floor. I hesitated, and then continued to my room. I opened the door as quietly as I could, in case she could hear my movements as I could hear hers. I didn't want to wake her and I didn't want her to know I'd been drinking with Fen. I lay on the bed in my clothes and stared up at the white swirled plaster. It was silent. I hoped she'd managed to fall asleep. My bed felt more comfortable than it had the previous nights and despite the slight spinning, Fen had been right: the cognac was going to allow me to sleep. I drifted down into it.

I awoke to pounding. Louder, and louder still. Then her door opening. All I could hear were footsteps and the low buzz of voices, first in the doorway then all over the small room. As their voices grew stronger their feet moved faster, back and forth above me. Something hit the floor hard. My body was on the stairs then pounding on her door before my mind caught up.

'Your boyfriend's here,' I heard Fen say.

'Let me in.'

A man across the hall said, 'Belt up, will you?"

The door opened.

Nell was in her nightgown at the end of the bed.

'Are you hurt?'

'I'm fine,' she said. 'Please, let's not get thrown out of here.'

'Nellie wants to go to the police. Get me thrown in the calaboose. Maybe make you her next houseboy. But you can bloody well forget that.' He bent over to light a cigarette. 'Natives kill natives. No one's going to put *me* behind bars for that. And the flute—it's not exactly the frieze of the fucking Parthenon and nobody cared how Elgin got that except for a few sentimental Greeks.'

'I want the governor of the station to know there could be trouble between the Mumbanyo and the Tam, that's all.' Her voice was thin, alien to me.

'Nell,' I said.

She shook her head fiercely at my tone. 'Please, go to bed, Bankson. Take Fen and go.'

Without a fight Fen followed me out of the room.

When we got down to the second floor I said, 'What happened up there?'

'Nothing. Marital argy-bargy.'

I grabbed him and shoved him against the wall. His body was completely relaxed, as if this were something he was used to. 'What was that noise I heard up there? What hit the ground?'

'Her duffel. It was on the bed and I chucked it to the floor. Christ.' He waited for me to let him go then opened his door.

I returned to my room and stood for a long time in the center of it, watching the ceiling, but I heard nothing the rest of the night.

Outside my room next morning was a hotel laundry bag, half full. I brought it to my bed and took out the items one by one: a pair of leather shoes, a tortoiseshell comb, a silver bracelet, her wrinkled blue dress. At the bottom, a note for me.

> You have already done so much that I am ashamed to ask for one thing more. Will you give these things to Teket when you go back, and ask him to take them to Lake Tam the next time he visits? The bracelet is for Bani, the comb for Wanji, the dress for Sali, and the shoes for Malun. Ask him to say to Malun that she is tight in my stomach. Teket's cousin will know how to say it.
>
> Please let me go. Don't say anything more or it will make it worse. I am going to try and fix what I can.

At the quai, the ship hovered over everything. I helped with their bags, chased down a porter.

'Last time to tie her shoes,' Fen said. His flute was wrapped and tied tight, and he set it down gently to shake my hand.

I turned to her. Her face looked small and rigid and miserable. We hugged. I held her close and too long. 'I don't want to let you go,' I breathed in her ear.

But I did. I let her go. And they boarded their ship.

27

I returned to the Kiona. Teket punished me for my long disappearance by not talking to me for the first two days. A few of the old women harangued me on his behalf, but no one else seemed bothered, and the children resumed their habit of following me around, begging to try on my pig's tusk and waiting for me to discard something—an empty tin, an old typewriter ribbon, a used tube of toothpaste—for their amusement. The rains had finally come and the river was high but hadn't flooded over yet. The women went out to their gardens in pointy leaf ponchos and the children made what looked like cities in the mud.

They held the Wai they had promised me. Despite all my interviews, my hundreds of questions to hundreds of Kiona about this ceremony, I had got it all wrong. I had missed the complexity of it. Part bawdy, part historical, and part tragic, the ceremony elicited a greater range of emotions than I had realized the first time round. There was a reenactment of their crocodile origins and their cannibal past. Ancestors were brought back to life briefly as their clay death masks were worn by their descendants. Women in war paint and penis gourds chased men in reed skirts till they got them pinned down, then they scraped their bare buttocks on the men's legs—the ultimate Kiona insult—which made the audience cry with laughter. I sat with Teket and his family and took as many

notes on their reactions as I did on the ceremony itself. That
night I stayed up late, leaning against my gum tree and writing
Nell a fifteen-page letter she wouldn't receive until summer.

Two days later, I left.

I'd arranged for Minton to pick me up, take me to Lake
Tam, then drop me in Angoram, from where I would make
arrangements to get back to Sydney. Teket agreed to come
with me to the lake and stay on with his cousin for a visit.

Minton arrived early and in good spirits, until Teket
climbed into the boat after we'd loaded it up with my bags.

'Ho there,' he said. 'None of them on my boat.'

I was glad I hadn't paid him yet. 'I'll get Robby then.'
Robby was the more expensive driver. I began hoisting my
belongings off the pinnace.

'He can't sit back there where the ladies sit.'

'He'll sit where he bloody likes.'

Most likely Teket had understood exactly how the conversation had gone, but he didn't let on. We sat where the ladies
sat, the Black Opal laundry bag of gifts between us.

It had been difficult to tell Teket what had happened. He'd
known Xambun from visits to his cousin. I told him Fen's
explanations for why Xambun was shot and not him. Teket
said he'd never heard of anyone trying to get killed—they
did not have a word for suicide in Kiona—and he scoffed
at the idea of a white man thinking he could be invisible. If
the Mumbanyo had shot at Fen, Teket said, the whole village

would have been rounded up and put in jail. Of course they had aimed for Xambun.

Minton had never been to Lake Tam. We guided him through the canals. I'd worried that he'd balk at pushing his boat through them but he kept saying, 'This is fucking loony, mate,' with a tremendous grin on his face. Then we were out on the lake and his boat sped us across the black water much faster than my canoe ever had, and I wasn't prepared to arrive so quickly.

The lake was high, the beach only a thin strip near the grasses. The mosquitoes were much worse now. Clouds of them swarmed the minute the boat slowed. I could see the tip of their house. It seemed impossible that Nell would not be behind the blue-and-white cloth door.

The sound of the boat had attracted attention. I helped Minton tie up while Teket was greeted warmly by his cousin and her family. She was not someone who had come to Nell in the mornings and Nell had said she was shy, conscious of her foreignness, and avoided being interviewed. I became aware of a line of older men on the road above, looking down at us. They were not armed with spears or bows, I noted with relief. Teket saw them, too. We exchanged glances, then he sent his cousin to find Malun and the others.

It was understood that I was not welcome in the village, and Teket waited with me on the beach. After a long time, they came. They walked close together, Malun in the middle, her face stiff and grim. She and Sali were covered in mourning mud.

We all squatted in the sand as I gave out Nell's gifts.

Bani pushed the silver bracelet up tight on his arm above his elbow, and Wanji ran off with his comb, screaming out to his friends as he tore up the path. Sali gasped when I pulled the dress out of the bag, as if I were pulling out Nell herself. She put it in the sand beside her, but laid a hand on top, as if it might walk away. She and Malun each had a crusted scab at the top of a finger stub, cut off at the middle knuckle for Xambun.

I handed Malun the bag that held the shoes. After a long while she tipped her head in to see but did not bring them out. Her gaze remained hard. I was glad Nell was not here to see it. I asked Teket's cousin to tell them that Nell was so very sorry, that she wanted to make amends in any way she could. I told Malun she was tight in Nell-Nell's stomach. At this Malun's face gave way but she remained still and did not wipe away her tears that cut dark lines through the dry mud.

Bani asked to speak with me privately. We walked a few yards down the beach. With the English Nell had taught him he said, ' Fen is bad man.' Then, in case I didn't understand, he said it in pidgin, which I didn't know he knew: 'Em nogut man.'

I nodded but he wasn't satisfied so he switched back to English. 'He break her.'

It was true, then. I did the tally, too late, of all the broken things: her ankle, her glasses, her typewriter.

When I left, Malun was standing in her brown shoes and Sali was wearing her dress like a scarf, and the men were still standing on the bluff above.

Teket gave us a push out. We called our last farewells to each other. Neither of us felt like it was a real goodbye, and it wasn't. I would return to the Kiona many times.

Minton put the boat in reverse and we turned slowly away from the beach. I'd wire my mother for more money, I decided, and go directly to New York from Sydney. I would not wait. The boat gained speed and skimmed fast to the canals.

'Not the most hospitable tribe, are they?' Minton said. 'Those boongs up on the embankment looked like they'd cark you given half a chance.'

28

3/? I have done it. Full fathom five it lies. Hiding out here in the 3rd class library for the time being. Strange how a ship was our doing and now our undoing. Let him rage. Let him rage across the oceans. But he will rage alone. I am getting off tomorrow at Aden. Doubling back to Sydney. He is wine and bread and deep in my stomach.

29

When I reached Sydney, I found there was no boat coming in for a fortnight, so I kicked around there impatiently, setting up an office of sorts at the Black Opal, but getting no work done. I frequented a pub called the Cat and Fiddle far too early and too often. My mother cabled more money, though I didn't tell her that I would see her only for the two days the boat was docked at Liverpool, that I was going to go on to America.

The day before I sailed, I worked up the courage to go back and see the bark paintings at the Art Gallery. I simply wanted to walk where we had walked, stand where we had stood. She would have nearly reached the Continent by now, I calculated. On the way I passed the shop where I'd gotten the plasters, and the *New Yorker* restaurant. Across the lobby of the museum I heard my name.

'My, my, someone's taken a bath.'

It was Mrs. Swale, my dinner partner at the Iyneses'. She took my arm and never looked back at the group she'd come in with. I was aware of the scent of her, not the humid root smell of Kiona women or Nell by the time I met her, but an inorganic smell meant to cover it all up.

We went up the stairs to the exhibit. She began her questioning: How long had I been here, when would I leave, not tomorrow, couldn't I change my ticket? And then just before we entered the hall, she looked at me quite gravely, more gravely than I expected her face to be able to look. 'I was so sorry to hear about your friend's wife.'

'What do you mean?' My lips went all rubbery in an instant. In fact my whole body seemed to be pulling away from me.

She covered her mouth and shook her head and with an intake of breath she said she was sorry, she thought for sure I'd know.

'Know what?' I said loudly into the vast room.

Hemorrhaging. Just before they reached Aden. Mrs. Swale put her hand over mine and I wanted to swat it away.

'Did you know she was pregnant?'

'Twins,' I said before I turned away from her. 'She thought it might be twins.'

I went to see Claire directly from the museum. She wasn't home and I waited for several hours in her enormous house, listening to clocks chime and dogs bark and servants hustle about as if the world were on fire. When she did arrive and saw my face she dropped her parcels and called out for whiskey. I'd held out a faint hope that Isabel Swale, with her poor aptitude, had gotten it all wrong, but Claire doused it within seconds. 'They couldn't stop the bleeding.' She paused, guessing how much more I could handle. I held her gaze and took in a steady breath. 'The ghastly thing is, Fen insisted on a sea burial. Her parents are apoplectic. Think he's hiding something. They've started proceedings against him and the ship's captain. It's all been such a drama.' She sounded quite bored by Nell's death.

She poured me another drink and in the light breeze of her movements I smelled again the manufactured smell of these women. Her husband, she told me quite pointedly, was away for several days.

All I wanted was to call a cab and be delivered to my room. But I could not seem to ask for that, and sat in silence, willing my glass to stop shaking as I lifted it to my lips. I couldn't seem to pull air into my lungs. I thought of Fen and Nell meeting on the boat: I'm having trouble breathing, she'd said. And then I broke down. No Southerner, Claire did her best to comfort me with palaver and awkward pats on the arm, but as soon as I could stand, she put me in a car that took me back down to the city.

30

On my ship, the SS *Vedic*, I walked the decks, stood at the rails, spoke to no one except the sea. There were times when I thought I saw her out there on the water, sitting cross-legged, surprised and grinning as if I'd just walked into the room. There were other times when the water was black as space, sinister in its enormity. She was out there. I did not know where. Fen had dumped her in the sea. She couldn't even swim. Facts I still only half believed. I leaned over the rail and hollered out at the emptiness. I didn't mind who heard. I'd hoped John and Martin, whose voices had always come to me when I was cracking up, would chime in but they were silent, too sorry for me, or too appalled, to make their usual fun.

We crossed into the Java Sea. The moon swelled to full.

Once, Nell had told me, there was a Mumbanyo man who wanted to kill the moon. He had discovered his wife bled each month and accused her of having another husband. She laughed and told him all women were married to the moon. I will kill this moon, the man said, and he got in his canoe and after many days he came to the tree from which the moon, tied to the highest branch by raffia string, jumped into the sky. Come down here so I can kill you, the man said to the moon, for you have stolen my wife. The moon laughed. Every woman is my wife first, he said. So in fact you stole this wife from me. This only made the man angrier and he climbed the tree to the highest branch and pulled at the raffia string. It would not move so he began to climb the string toward the moon. Soon his arms grew heavy and though he had climbed far from the tree he still was no closer to the moon. Let go now, the moon said. And the man, who had no more strength left, let go and fell directly into his canoe and paddled home to share his wife, as all men did, with the moon.

A tall brooding slightly unhinged Englishman is bound to capture the romantic imagination of some girl, and there was one from Shropshire who followed me around for a week or so, but she came to understand that my dark silences were never going to bloom into confessions of love, and took up with an Irish soldier.

My boat pulled in and out of Colombo, Bombay, Aden. A day out from Suez, I discovered the notes from our Grid stuffed into a corner of one of the suitcases. I had no memory of putting them there. In fact I was certain I hadn't. I smoothed them all out on the walnut desk in my stateroom. It was the work of madness, the oily crumpled pages covered in three different scrawls, but I was mad still, and set to work. I wrote the monograph quickly, faster than I've ever written anything. They were both there with me as I wrote, both of them, advising me, heckling me, contradicting me, mocking me, and, finally, approving. I wrote with more conviction than I'd ever had in my life about anything. I wanted to get it right for her, wanted to hold on to those moments on Lake Tam in any way I could. I thought the writing would last the rest of the journey, but I was done by Genoa and posted it from there. I had signed all three of our names to it.

Oceania took it for their next issue, and it was included in several anthologies published the following year. The Grid, for a time, became a staple in classrooms in several countries. In 1941 though I learned that Eugen Fischer in Berlin had included its German translation in the reading lists he created for the Third Reich. He had added a coda, claiming Germans to be Northern, the unyielding Northern temperament to be superior, and our Grid to be further proof of the necessity of the Nazi racial hygiene program. That the monograph was in the company of works by Mendel and Darwin was cold comfort. If I had not known of this list, perhaps I would not have been so willing to offer up my knowledge of the Sepik for the purpose of war when the OSS contacted me, perhaps I would not have helped to rescue those three American spies in Kamindimimbut. And perhaps that entire Olimbi village would not have been slaughtered. So much, in the end, for all my attempts at amends.

After Genoa we stopped in Gibraltar and, finally, Liverpool.

Strange how you can pick out in a crowd, from a distance of eighty yards and two and a half years, the one familiar shape, the slant of white hair, the hands covering the mouth.

All those tough, no-nonsense letters, threats of disinheritance, lectures on the necessity of hard science, and my mother was heavy and sobbing in my arms.

'She never thought you'd make it back,' her friend who'd driven her up to Liverpool explained. 'She had terrible dreams.'

I wasn't much better than a pole, holding my mother up on that packed quai as all those passengers I never met bumped past us on their way into other arms. I had spoken only to the ocean for forty-seven days, hadn't slept since Sydney. My mother took ahold of herself, told me I looked awful, and led me to her friend's automobile, where she sat with me in the backseat and held my hand. I hadn't written her a word of what had happened, yet she seemed to know it all. The tar and soot smell of England was back in my nostrils, the cold damp already settling in my bones. The SS *Vedic* was lit up now in the dusk. Morning after next it would begin its passage without me across another swath of emptiness to New York. Through the windscreen I had a last look at the sea, which was rumpled and agitated, a thick muscle that would hold on tight to everything it swallowed.

31

I have only been to America once. It is not easy to avoid the place, but for years I managed it. I declined invitations, turned down teaching posts. But when they sent me the announcement of the opening of the Peoples of the Pacific Hall at the American Museum of Natural History in the spring of 1971, which had a photograph of a ceremonial house on the front and a quote from my most recent book about Kiona below it, I felt obliged to make the journey.

I was given a private viewing before the event. Viewing me and my responses as we padded along on carpeted floors were the director of the museum, the president of its board, and several big donors. There were Balinese shadow puppets, a Maori pataka, Moro armor. There was a diorama of a Solomon Island village with a copy of *The Children of Kirakira* on a shelf behind it, overlooking the scene like a god.

'And here,' said the director as we turned a corner, 'is your particular part of the world.' It surprised me, a whole large annex devoted to the Sepik River tribes. Years earlier I'd donated my few Kiona-made possessions to the museum, never expecting to see them again, and there they all were now, pinned and labeled and under glass like Aunt Dottie's beetles: my painted coconut cups, my stick and snail navigational chart, my shell money, the few clay figures given to me upon my departure. The pages from a November 1933 issue of *Oceania* containing the monograph about the Grid was under glass as well, torn to shreds as I had requested. Beside it was a placard noting the serendipity of the monograph's three authors having met in Angoram on Christmas Eve, 1932, our theory's misappropriation by the Nazis, my subsequent refusal of all reprinting requests, and my entreaties that it be permanently removed from all syllabi around the globe. According to the synopsis, those efforts had only enhanced its popularity. Beside the shredded *Oceania* article were my books and the book Nell's publisher had shaped from Nell's New Guinea notes, which was even more successful than her first. Another placard gave an account of Nell's death at sea, Fen's disappearance, and my long career. Though the museum had no Sepik artifacts directly from Nell or Fen, a young anthropologist had recently retraced their steps and brought back a number of items from the Anapa, Mumbanyo, and Tam.

Fen had indeed vanished. No one I know has heard from him in all these years. The only person ever to claim a sighting was Evans-Pritchard, who thought he saw him on the Omo River in Ethiopia in the late thirties, but when he called out Fen's name, the man flinched and moved swiftly away.

Tears are not endless, I repeated to myself. That was how I made the long walk past these display cases, past an enormous blowup of the photograph Fen had taken of Nell and me with my big suitcase and his pipe and hat and sago fronds across our shoulders. I kept us moving swiftly. It was the only way to get through it. I paused, however, when I got to a Tam death mask. Mud had been smoothed on top of the bone to refashion the face, hair taken from a living head and glued on top. The mud had dried beige, and white warrior stripes were painted down the nose and across the cheeks and around the lips. In the socket of each eye was a small oval cowrie shell, underside up, the long slit with its toothed edges making an excellent likeness to a shut eye with lashes. Five more cowrie shells were placed across the forehead like a crown. It was this line of shells that caught my eye. Something irregular. The one in the middle was bigger, not a shell in fact but a button, a perfectly round ivory button embedded in this mud forehead. I reached for it. My hand slammed into the glass. It did not shatter, but it made a loud bang, which was followed by a sudden silence all around me.

'See someone you know in there?' one of the donors said, and the others laughed nervously.

Caught in the holes of the button were tufts of pale blue thread. I forced myself on to the next display. It was only a button. It was only a bit of thread. From a wrinkled blue dress I had once undone.

Acknowledgments

While this is a work of fiction, it was initially inspired by a moment described in Jane Howard's 1984 biography *Margaret Mead: A Life* and my subsequent reading of anything I could locate about anthropologists Margaret Mead, Reo Fortune, and Gregory Bateson, and their few months together in 1933 on the Sepik River of what was then called the Territory of New Guinea. I have borrowed from the lives and experiences of these three people, but have told a different story.

Most of the tribes and villages here are fictional. You cannot find the Tam or the Kiona on a map, though I have used details from the real tribes Mead, Fortune, and Bateson were studying at the time: the Tchambuli (now called the Chambri), the Iatmul, the Mundugumor, and the Arapesh. The book I call *Arc of Culture* is modeled on Ruth Benedict's *Patterns of Culture*.

The following books helped me immeasurably in my research: *Naven* by Gregory Bateson; *With a Daughter's Eye: A Memoir of Margaret Mead and Gregory Bateson* by Mary Catherine Bateson; *Patterns of Culture* by Ruth Benedict; *The Last Cannibals* by Jens Bjerre; *Return to Laughter* by Elenore Smith Bowen; *One Hundred Years of Anthropology* edited by J. O. Brew; *The Way of All Flesh* by Samuel Butler; *To Cherish the World: Selected Letters of Margaret Mead* edited by Margaret M. Caffrey and Patricia A. Francis; *Sepik River Societies: A Historical*

Ethnography of the Chambri and Their Neighbors by Deborah Gewertz; *Women in the Field: Anthropological Experiences* edited by Peggy Golde; *Margaret Mead: A Life* by Jane Howard; *Papua New Guinea Phrasebook* by John Hunter; *Kiki: Ten Thousand Years in a Lifetime; An Autobiography from New Guinea* by Albert Maori Kiki; *Margaret Mead and Ruth Benedict: The Kinship of Women* by Hilary Lapsley; *Gregory Bateson: The Legacy of a Scientist* by David Lipset; *Argonauts of the Western Pacific* by Bronislaw Malinowski; *Rain and Other South Sea Stories* by Somerset Maugham; *The Mundugumor* by Nancy McDowell; *Blackberry Winter: My Early Years* by Margaret Mead; *Coming of Age in Samoa* by Margaret Mead; *Cooperation and Competition Among Primitive Peoples* edited by Margaret Mead; *Growing Up in New Guinea* by Margaret Mead; *Letters from the Field, 1925–1975* by Margaret Mead; *Sex and Temperament: In Three Primitive Societies* by Margaret Mead; *Four Corners: A Journey into the Heart of Papua New Guinea* by Kira Salak; *Malinowski, Rivers, Benedict, and Others: Essays on Culture and Personality* edited by George W. Stocking Jr.; *Observers Observed: Essays on Ethnographic Fieldwork* edited by George W. Stocking Jr.; *Village Medical Manual: A Layman's Guide to Health Care in Developing Countries—Volume II: Diagnosis and Treatment* by Mary Vanderkooi MD.

I am grateful to the following people for their careful and insightful reading of earlier drafts of this book: Tyler Clements, Susan Conley, Sara Corbett, Caitlin Gutheil, Anja Hanson, Debra Spark, my sister Lisa, my extraordinary agent Julie Barer, William Boggess, Gemma Purdy, and my beloved, brilliant, and wise editor Elisabeth Schmitz. I'm also grateful to Morgan Entrekin, Deb Seager, Charles Woods, Katie Raissian, Amy Hundley, Judy Hottensen, and everyone at Grove Atlantic. Liza Bakewell's keen anthropological eye on a later draft was invaluable. A big thank-you to the Inn by the Sea, where I finished the final-final edits in cut-rate bliss. And another to Cornelia Walworth, who brought me to the bookstore that day.

A special, perpetual thanks to my husband, Tyler, and our daughters, Calla and Eloise. All my love to you.